Puffin Books

NASTY!

There's this woman who lives somewhere in London who tells the most amazing stories. It all started when I met her in a pub at the Elephant and Castle. She told me about this giant flea that had terrorized the London Underground. After that, I kept bumping into her wherever I went, and each time she'd tell me a story that was even nastier than the last one. If it wasn't fleas it was killer wasps, grizzly bears or mad old women with sinister powers.

So let me give you a word of warning: what you are about to read could make you feel quite peculiar . . .

This collection of seven nasty stories contains three completely new ones specially written for Puffin.

Illustrated by Jon Riley

NASTY!

Michael Rosen

Puffin Books

PUFFIN BOOKS

Published by the Penguin Group
27 Wrights Lane, London W8 5TZ, England
Viking Penguin Inc., 40 West 23rd Street, New York, New York 10010, USA
Penguin Books Australia Ltd, Ringwood, Victoria, Australia
Penguin Books Canada Ltd, 2801 John Street, Markham, Ontario, Canada L3R 1B4
Penguin Books (NZ) Ltd, 182–190 Wairau Road, Auckland 10, New Zealand

Penguin Books Ltd, Registered Offices: Harmondsworth, Middlesex, England

The first four stories in *Nasty!* (together with two others)
were published by the Longman Group Ltd 1982

We are grateful to the ILEA English Centre for an adapted version of
'The Bakerloo flea'. The story first appeared in *Teachers' Writing*.

This Puffin edition, with three new stories, published 1984
10 9 8 7 6 5 4

Photoset in Linotron Goudy by
Rowland Phototypesetting Ltd, Bury St Edmunds, Suffolk
Printed and bound in Great Britain by
Cox & Wyman Ltd, Reading

Contents

The Bakerloo flea

Not long ago I was in a pub round the Elephant and Castle, and I got talking to a woman, an oldish woman. And we were talking about this and that, and she said she used to be a cleaner down the Underground. I didn't know, but it seems as if every night after the last tube, they switch the electric current off and teams of night-cleaners go through the Underground, along the tunnels, cleaning up all the muck, rubbish, fag ends and stuff that we chuck on to the lines. They sweep out between the lines on one station, and then, in a gang of about six or seven, walk on to the next station along the lines in the tunnels.

Anyway this woman (I don't know her name), she says to me:

'Did you ever hear talk of the Bakerloo flea?'

'Bakerloo flea?' I said. 'No, no, never.'

'Well,' she said, 'you know there are rats down there – down the Underground? Hundreds of 'em. And the thing is,' she said, 'is that some of them have grown enormous. Huge great big things.'

'I've heard of them,' I said. 'Super rats.'

'Right,' she says. 'Now you tell me,' she says, 'what lives on rats? Fleas, right? Fleas. So – the bigger the rats the bigger the fleas. Stands to reason. These rats, they feed on all the old garbage that people throw down on the lines. It's amazing what people throw away, you know.'

She told me they found a steak down there once, lipstick, a bowler hat, beads, a box of eggs and hundreds and hundreds of sweets – especially Maltesers and those balls of bubble gum you get out of slot machines.

Anyway, the rats eat these, get big, and it seems that one day they were working the Bakerloo Line – Elephant and Castle to Finchley Road – and just before Baker Street one of the women in the gang was looking ahead, and she screamed out:

'Look – look – what's that?' Up in front was a great, grey, spiky thing with huge hairy legs and big jaws. It was as big as a big dog – bigger.

And the moment she screamed, it jumped away from them, making a sort of grating, scraping noise. Well, they were scared stiff. Scared stiff. But they had to finish the job, so they carried on up the line to Finchley Road. But they didn't see it again that night or the next, or the next.

Some of them thought they'd imagined it, because it can get very spooky down there. They sing and shout a lot she told me, and tell saucy jokes, not fit for my ears.

Anyway, about a fortnight later, at the same place – just before Baker Street on the Bakerloo Line – suddenly one of them looks up and there it was again. A great, big, grey, spiky thing with long legs and big jaws.

'It's a flea, sure to God it's a flea,' one of them said.

The moment it heard this, again it jumped. Again, they heard this scraping, grating sound, and it disappeared down the tunnel – in the dark. They walked on, Baker Street, St John's Wood, Swiss Cottage, to Finchley Road. Nothing.

Anyway – this time they had a meeting. They decided it *was* a flea, a gigantic flea, and it must have grown up from a family of fleas that had lived for years and years growing bigger and bigger, sucking the blood of all the fat rats down there.

So they decided that it was time to tell one of the high-ups in London Transport, or they wouldn't go down there any more.

For a start off, no one'd believe them.

'Just a gang of women seeing things in the dark,' the supervisor said.

Right! One of them had a bright idea. She said:

'I'll tell you what we'll do – we'll tell them that we're coming out on strike, and we'll tell the papers about the flea, the Bakerloo flea. It'll be a huge scandal – no one'll dare go by tube, it'll be a national scandal.'

So they threatened the manager with this, and this time the high-ups really moved. They were so scared the story might get out, and they'd be blamed, and one of *them* would lose their jobs.

So for a start they stopped all cleaning on the Bakerloo Line, and one of the high-ups went down the tunnel with the women. You can just see it, can't you? Four in the morning, a gang of six women with feather dusters, and one of the bowler hat and briefcase brigade walking down the tunnel on the hunt for the Bakerloo flea. Sounded incredible to me.

Anyway, it seems as if they came round that same corner just before Baker Street and the women had gone quiet and the bloke was saying: 'If this is a hoax, if this is a trick . . .' when they heard that awful, hollow, scraping noise.

At first they couldn't see it, but then – there it was – not *between* the lines this time – *on* the lines – a gigantic flea. No question, that's what it was.

Well, he took one look at it, and next moment he was backing off.

'Back, ladies, back. Back, ladies!'

Of course *he* was more scared than they were. Terrified. But he was even more terrified when one of the women let out this scream. Not because *she* was scared, but to scare off the flea. And it worked. It jumped. Right out of sight.

Well there was no carrying on up the line that night.

'Back, ladies, back,' was all he could say, and back they went.

Next thing they knew, they were all called into an office with a carpet and the Queen on the wall. And there was a whole gang of these men.

First thing, one of them says, they weren't to let anyone

know of this, no one at all must ever hear of what they had all seen. There was no point in letting a panic develop. Anyway, next he says:

'We haven't let the grass grow under our feet. We've got a scientist with us.'

And then the scientist, he says:

'I've got this powder. Deadly flea powder. All you need to do is spread this up and down the Bakerloo Line, and there'll be no more trouble with this flea thing.'

Well, the woman in the pub – I never found out her name – said:

'So who's going to spread this stuff about down there? The Army?'

'No,' the man said. 'We don't see any need for that. You,' he says, 'you.'

'So that's a fine one,' the woman said to me. 'First of all they said it was just a bunch of women afraid of the dark, then they send Tarzan in pinstripes down there and he can't get out fast enough, and now it's us that has to spread this flea powder.'

'Well,' she said, 'we knew it wouldn't be any good anyway. Flea powder never is.'

They took it down there, threw it about between Regents Park and Baker Street and Swiss Cottage – while up above, in the big houses, ambassadors from all over the world slept soundly in their beds. They told them not to go down for a week, and not to breathe a word of it to anyone.

'They were more scared of a story in the papers than we were of the flea,' she said.

It hadn't attacked anyone, no one had seen it there in daytime, so down they went. But there it was again – sitting there just before Baker Street, with some of the powder sticking to the hairs on its legs. But this time, instead of hopping away down the line, it turned and faced them. They turned and ran, and then it leaped. It leaped at the women, and they ran back down the tunnel to Regents Park. This great, grey flea was trying to get at them.

'We screamed,' she said, 'we really screamed, but it was after us, 'cos you see that damned flea powder hadn't killed the flea – it had killed the rats. It was starving for fresh blood. Probably *mad* for blood, by now,' she said. 'We ran and ran and the flea was hopping – but it was hitting the roof of the tunnel, it was so mad to get at us. There was this terrible scraping sound of its shell on the roof of the tunnel, and it'd fall back onto the lines. So we could move faster than it. We rushed back to Regents Park, and calls went up and down the line and all over the system to lock the gates on every station and seal the system. Seal off the Underground system of London. Well, it was about four o'clock – two hours to go before a million people would be down there.

'What were they going to do? Upstairs in the office they were in a blind panic. They could've done something about it earlier, instead of fobbing us off. They couldn't call in the Army without telling the Minister, and if they told the Minister, he'd tell the Prime Minister, and all the high-ups would get the sack. So they had this plan to turn the current on, and run the maintenance train at high speed through the tunnel from Finchley Road to the Elephant and Castle, in the hope that it would get killed beneath the wheels of the train, or smashed against the buffers at the Elephant.

'They did it. They sent it through. Of course *that* didn't work. We knew it wouldn't work. Anyone that's lived with a flea knows you can't squash fleas – you've got to crack 'em. They're hard, rock hard.

'After the maintenance man ran the maintenance train through, they went down to the gates at Regents Park, and they stood and listened, and from down below they could hear the grating, scraping noise of its shell on its legs. Of course, it was obvious now why it had stuck to this stretch of the line all the time. Some of the juiciest rubbish was in the bins round those posh parts, so you got the biggest rats, so that was where you got the great Bakerloo flea.

'So now they had less than two hours to get rid of the

flea, or leave it for a day and run the risk of letting a million people down into the tunnels to face a flea, starving, starving for blood, or shutting the whole system down and telling everyone to go by bus.

'Well you know what happened?' she said. '*We* did it. *We* got rid of it.'

'You did?'

'Yes, we did it.

'Vera's old man worked on the dustcarts for Camden Council. She knew how to kill the flea. It was Vera's plan that what we'd do was go down, actually down onto the line at Oxford Circus with dustbin lids, banging them with brushes and broom handles, and drive the flea back up the line to Finchley Road where the Bakerloo Line comes out of the tunnel into the open air. And at Finchley Road, Vera's old man and his gang would have a couple of carts backed up into the tunnel. And that's what we did. We got driven to Vera's place to get her old man up, on to his mates' places to get them up, then they went to the Council builder's yard to get boards, builders' planks. We got the lids off the bins, and down we went. Oxford Circus, Regents Park, Baker Street, St John's Wood, Swiss Cottage, Finchley Road, and we shouted and we banged, and we banged and we shouted every step of the way.

'We saw it just once at Swiss Cottage waiting for us, but we walked together holding the lids up in front of us like shields, and it was as if it knew it couldn't get at us this time, 'cos it turned – it had just room to turn in the tunnel – and as we came up to Finchley Road still banging and shouting, it leaped – not at us, but at one of the carts.

Alongside it was the other one, between the wheels were the boards, some of them stacked up to block off all the gaps. The flea was trapped between us with our lids and the back of the dustcarts. It leaped, it hit the roof of the tunnel, just like it did when it chased us. We shouted and banged. It leaped again. This time we had it. It was in the back of the dustcart.

We kept up the banging and the shouting. We got as near to the back of the dustcart as we could. We could see it there, every hair of its legs, and Vera shouts:

'"Turn it on, Bob, turn it on," and Bob turned on the masher (they call it "The Shark"), in the back of his cart. And it bit into the back of that flea like giant nails crunching through eggshells. The smell was revolting. Bit by bit, the flea was dragged into the cart. We could see it as it went: first its body, then its legs. I'll never forget the sight of those huge hairy legs twitching about in the back of Bob's cart, Vera shouting:

'"You've got him, love, you've got him!"

'He had, too. That was that. That was the end of the Bakerloo flea. But do you know, when we got up to the top, that load from head office were there. They were crying, crying out of relief, crying their eyes out. Twenty minutes later, hundreds and thousands of people were down there, off to work, none the wiser. They didn't know about any flea, any Bakerloo flea. They don't even know we go down there every night cleaning up their mess for them. Of course, head office made us promise never to breathe a word of it. We promised.

'Vera said:

'"What's it worth to you?"

'He said:

'"Your honour. Your word. And your word's your honour."

'And they gave us a week's extra holiday tagged on to August Bank Holiday that year.'

She told me I was the first person she'd ever told the story to, and told me never to tell anyone. The scandal would be terrible. I don't know whether to believe her or not.

A plague of wasps in winter

You remember the woman who told me the story of the
Bakerloo flea? Well, I didn't see her again for ages, until
one day, I was in the park round my way in Hackney, and
suddenly – there she was.

'You don't live round here, do you?' I said to her.

'No,' she says, 'but my son does, now he's married, and I
like to come across and see them once in a while – when I
can afford it.'

'I bet you don't remember what you told me, the last
time we met,' I said.

'What was that?' she says.

'That story – that story about the giant flea that lived
down the Underground. I've told other people that story,
and no one believes it. For a start the Bakerloo Line
doesn't go where you said it went. Where you said it went
is the Jubilee Line.'

'Do me a favour, love,' she says, 'it did for fifty years. If
London Transport happened to want to run their posh
new Jubilee Line through the old Bakerloo tunnels – then
that's their business. In my day, it was the Bakerloo Line.
In my day, it was the Bakerloo flea.'

I gave her a look as if to say, Now pull the other one!
But as I was just hanging about, and it was a nice day, I
said to her:

'Still, I don't suppose any other amazing things have happened to you, have they?'

'Now that's funny you should say that,' she said, 'because I was thinking. You know this summer has been a real devil for wasps, hasn't it?'

'Yeah,' I said.

'Well, it put me in mind of one time, some years back now, when it wasn't the summer we were bothered by them – it was the winter!'

'Go on!' I said.

'My son wasn't long married, and his wife – Eileen – was expecting, so I used to come across and see them more often in those days, and stay over the weekend. They were living in the GLC flats down by the Hackney Marshes. Just next to the River Lea.'

'I know,' I said, 'the Kingsmead.'

'They're the ones,' she said.

'Well it was a devil of a winter that one,' she said, 'and all the harder because it'd come after a really nice summer. Now – and I know you're not going to believe your ears when I tell you this, even though it was such a devil of a winter – a very funny thing happened. They had a plague of wasps down there. No other word for it – a plague of wasps in winter! It was one of the most frightening, terrible things that I have ever seen, and it all happened just when Eileen was having the baby.'

'Don't tell me,' I said. 'Go on.'

'Well, I'll spare you the worst,' she says. 'But terrible things went on that winter. You can't imagine it. There we'd be, say, sitting indoors having our tea. Outside it'd be cold – raining maybe – and, like all of a sudden, you'd hear this buzzing. And you could never be sure whether it come from the windows, or under the table, or where. And then, maybe you'd look up, and there – from out the light-fitting – there'd come one, two, three, four, five, six, maybe ten wasps – one after another – crawling out. Then they'd drop onto the table, or begin to buzz round and round the room. They always acted like they were drunk – or drugged. They didn't know what they were doing. I didn't know what they were doing. I remember once they just fell straight into our tea things. They bobbed about in the tea, and crawled all over the sandwiches, and two landed in my son's hair.

'Now, my son has thick hair, really thick, wiry hair, and the moment those wasps landed, it was as if they knew they had a job of work to do. They set to work digging their way through his hair to get to his scalp. But that wasn't all. One landed on his collar as well. I saw it there – I can see it to this day – and, the next moment, it was creeping over the edge, and down his neck.

'"There's two of 'em in your hair," Eileen's shouting.

'"Never mind them," he shouts. "There's one coming down my neck."

'And he's struggling to get his jumper and shirt loose.

'"It's got me. It's got me. It's got me."

'He was really screaming now, and dancing around like a mad monkey tearing at his clothes. But he was afraid to pull them off himself, because they'd just squeeze the wasp harder against his skin.

'"Let me get at those two in your hair," Eileen yelled at him.

'"One's got me right on the chest, as well. They're

stinging me all over," he was yelling. "Get 'em out, get 'em out. I can't do it. *I* can't do it. Get me shirt off me back."

'Course, by now he was scared to get the jumper over his head, because that would just squash his hair down onto his head. Oh, it was terrifying to watch him. He was like a mad bull, and he was swearing something terrible.

'"Tear it off me, you two, will you," he says. "Don't stand there. They've got through to me head now."

'So Eileen grabbed the bread-knife off the table.

'"Stand still. For God's sake, stand still, love," she screams at him.

'So with two wasps stinging at his scalp and another down his neck, he froze. He stood stock still. And she hacked at the jumper with the bread-knife. I grabbed a chair, jumped up on it and tried to find the two of 'em that'd got tangled up in that hair of his. Talk about a needle in a haystack. Not that I was scared, mind. But my boy, he's allergic to wasp stings. They swell up something awful. Huge red lumps. And, last time it happened, the doctor said it would be all right so long as he didn't get stung too many times at once. But he didn't know how many times might be too many for my boy. It could be ten or it could be hundreds. We just didn't know. My boy just stood there, rooted to the spot, Eileen hacking at his jumper, and me going through his hair like a dog looking for fleas.

'"They're still stinging me," he says to me, through his teeth.

'Eileen tore that jumper apart, ripped his shirt and vest off, and the wasp just flopped off him on to the floor. With my bare fingers – and I can tell you I never dared do it before in my life – I pulled first the one, then the other wasp out of his hair. And as I pulled them out of his hair, I squeezed their heads. That's how I killed them. I squeezed their heads.

'Next day my boy's back looked like a sack of potatoes, and ooh, he *was* sick, I can tell you. He *was* sick. But, I tell you, what I saw was nothing to what others saw, or what got into the paper, or what people told you about round the flats, or up the new launderette. In the mornings, out shopping, you'd find yourself talking to people you didn't even know.

'"Did you get any last night?" someone'd say.

'"Only half a dozen in my bath. Come crawling up the overflow pipe while I was having my bath, didn't they?"

'There was people finding them underneath their pillows, in their saucepans, or blowing them out their hair-dryers. And when you met people in the street, the first thing they did was stand there showing you swollen fingers, swellings on their necks, or their lips, or even on their eyelids. Oh it was a terrible time for us all, I can tell you.'

I was amazed by all this and I told her so.

'But why didn't I ever hear about any of this?' I said.

'Oh,' she says, 'no one ever hears about what goes on down my boy's way. They used to call it the Land that God Forgot. I mean, you didn't hear about the Blackwall Tunnel disaster, either, did you?'

'Which one?' I asked. 'Every morning I have my local radio station on, and there's always someone saying, "All traffic's stuck in the Blackwall Tunnel, because a lorry's shed its load."'

'Well this one concerns them wasps,' she said. 'You see, people were going about saying awful things. Spiteful, hurtful things, putting the blame on immigrants. They were saying they'd brought the wasps over. They were saying they were coming over in the fruit and veg. I mean, in those days, I'd never seen some of the things that was turning up in the markets. It's different now. Eileen's next door neighbour, Charmaine – she's from Jamaica – she's cooked up some of it for us, and we've come to like it. Plantain and stuff. I remember once, though, going down Ridley Road Market and seeing what I thought were huge bananas. Enormous things. I daren't tell you the saucy comments people were making. And a friend of Charmaine turned to me and said, "Them's not banana – them's plantain." I felt so ignorant – you know what I mean?'

'And the Blackwall Tunnel?' I said.

'Yes, of course. Well you see, I remember sitting one Sunday evening with Charmaine's little girl Donna.

'"It ain't us, Aunty, we didn't bring them things with us, Aunty," she said. "I know because *I* know where they do come from, you see."

'"Of course you do, my love, of course you do," I said.

'"But I'm not saying," she says, "Because no one believes me."

'"No," I say, "No, now never you mind. You just run along and play with your brother, and let Aunty sit down for a bit."

'Well, she goes off, and I didn't think any more about it – until the Blackwall Tunnel disaster happened.'

'I've been waiting for that,' I said.

'Well,' she says, 'you know Tate and Lyle, the sugar people, Golden Syrup and the like? Well, they've got their works down by the river, and every day the men take out tanker lorries full of Golden Syrup.'

'What? Like petrol tankers full of Golden Syrup? Ooh, lovely,' I said.

'Yes. That's what the wasps thought,' she said.

'No one's quite sure what happened, but two of their fellers drove their tankers out the gates and as they turned into the Blackwall Tunnel there was some sort of collision. One of the fellers said afterwards that there was wasps in his cab driving him spare, but the other feller said that it wasn't the first bloke's fault. He said, "It was my fault." He'd felt his back wheels sliding out across the road like a skid on ice. But whatever happened, one tanker hit the other tanker in the back, and cracked open its tank.

The two lorries jammed up the Blackwall Tunnel.'

'I can guess what happened,' I said.

'I bet you can,' she said. 'And you'd be right. Syrup poured out all over the road. And worse still, it got into the cab and all over the feller in the tanker behind. After that, it was almost as if the wasps could tell each other the news – as if they could telephone each other up – because inside half an hour, the place was crawling with hundreds and thousands of wasps. They'd come for the syrup.

'We watched it on telly. We could see the arch, and the dark entrance to the tunnel, and every inch of those two tankers was crawling with wasps. There were thousands more buzzing around in the air. Then the man on the telly says very quiet, "The driver of the second tanker is still in the cab."'

'And what happened to the driver?' I asked.

'I don't want to say,' she said.

'How do you mean?'

'There are some things that it's better not talked about,' she said.

'Did he live?' I said.

'Yes and no,' she said. 'What was left of him lived.'

'But that's horrible,' I said.

'Yeah, and it took them a whole day to clear the mess up,' she said. 'The Fire Brigade came in with their fire engines and sprays and gas masks. They covered the place with some kind of foam. Poison foam that killed off the wasps in their thousands, and they had reports all the time on the telly and local radio. Expert this and expert that kept coming on – people who had been in Malaya, people who had been in Burma during the war – they all came on giving their two pennyworth. Because, now, it was all different, wasn't it?'

'How do you mean?' I asked.

'Well, so long as it was just the likes of us, on the estates, getting stung to hell and back, it was just another problem – like the drains is just another problem, or the gutters, or the rubbish piling up – but now, well . . . '

'Oh I get you,' I said, 'pictures of the lorry driver on the telly, and all that.'

'Not a bit of it. It was Tate and Lyle, they got scared. The wasps now knew where they were.'

'Who were?' I asked.

'Tate and Lyle. The wasps would come in and get 'em. Gobble up all the sugar. It didn't matter them stinging *us*. What mattered was that hundreds and thousands of wasps had got a whiff of all that sugar sitting there! I remember Charmaine saying it was never her folk that did that. She said Tate and Lyle have been bringing sugar into London from the West Indies since olden days. It was no immigrants that did that.'

'Never mind that,' I said. 'What happened? What happened?'

'Well, next thing was they made a minister. A Minister of Wasps, or something. And Tate and Lyle put up a reward. Thousands of pounds it was for anyone who could help find out where these wasps were coming from. You see, everyone knew how to kill wasps – whether it was me with my bare hands, or the Fire Brigade with their poisons and their foams. But what no one knew was *where the little devils were coming from.*

'Two or three times, they had a big thing on the telly with everyone from everywhere having their say. And that man with the glasses – I forget his name – he sat in the middle like a king. We all watched them. Donna used to come in while Charmaine did the late shift at work. Once, the man from Tate and Lyle was on with this puppet thing – Mr Cube it was – their mascot, and a person come on the programme, and said, "I think the wasps are coming from Wapping, coming from the docks or the wharves down there where the spices and raisins are stored."

'And we all shouted, "No, no, never! Rubbish! Take him off!" And then someone came on and said, "Somewhere there must be a giant wasp. A giant queen wasp. Maybe hundreds of giant queen wasps, lasting out the winter, away out of sight, keeping theirselves all snug and warm somewhere." And we were there saying, "Could be. He could be right, there, couldn't he?"

'After that, some people came and talked about some wasp traps and wasp poisons, but in the end, they all said that they had to find the queen.

'So the hunt was on, and we were getting desperate, I can tell you. Grown men were that afraid, some of 'em couldn't face getting themselves out of the house in the morning. Some people couldn't face going down to the shops, and sat indoors behind nets and netting draped all over the place. And so on the telly, on the next big programme, people came on trying to get that Tate and Lyle reward for catching the giant queen. They came on with all kinds of things – yellow beetles, dead bumble bees – and the experts kept saying, "No, no, no, that's not her." And Mr Cube kept saying, "No, no, no that's not her."

'It caught on everywhere, you know. Everyone was saying it. Once, we got the Sunday roast out the oven, put it on the table, and one of the kids took a look at it, and went "No, no, no that's not her." We did have our laughs I suppose. But anyway, you'll never guess who found those queens everyone was after?'

'No,' I said. 'I can't.'

'Donna,' she says.

'I don't believe it,' I said.

'Like I said, the hunt was on. There were more and more of the wasps about. There was Tate and Lyle on the verge of being gobbled out of their works, and losing a fortune or two. The hospitals were full of people who had been nearly stung to death. Hundreds of people were creeping round their houses thinking that just because twenty wasps had crawled out their wardrobe, the queen was in there. They probably burnt out more old buildings, sheds and fences that winter than what they tried to do to us in the blitz.'

'Yeah,' I said, 'And Donna?'

'Well, it was the third of these big telly programmes. Donna was in, Charmaine was out. Eileen, my boy, and the baby were out. It was a cold Sunday evening in January. So, me and Donna, we snuggled in together on the settee, and watched. This time they had the cameras out and about looking at different places where this queen wasp might be.

'A man came on and swore blind that there was a nest of queens in a warehouse place where they were storing perm mixture – the stuff the hairdressers use to set hair.

'"They're not there, Aunty," Donna says. "The queens aren't there."

'And she was right. They went all over this perm factory, in and out the tanks, and up and down ladders, and in the end Mr Cube came on the telly and he said, "No, No, No. The queens are not there."

'I think the telly people were beginning to think it was all a bit of a joke. Well, put it this way, so long as the hunt for the queen wasp was on – they were happy. They had something to make telly programmes about, didn't they? I think they loved it. But, it wasn't like that for us.

'"It's not funny, is it?" Donna said.

'"No," I said, "it isn't."

'"Aunty. *I* know where the queens are," she told me again.

'"All right, where?" I said, listening this time.

'"In the Dump," she says.

'"What dump?" I say.

'"The Dump where we're not allowed to play. Only, our Neville does, and so do some of the other big boys."

'"Don't tell tales, Donna," I says.

'"The queens are in there, Aunty," she says.

'"Yes, I know they're in there, Donna love," I said, just to keep her quiet.

'The dump Donna was talking about was no ordinary dump. It was a huge site on the Marshes where they had drained the land. They dumped heaps and heaps of rubbish there all day long – and often long into the night under floodlights. And they had those huge rollers out pressing it all down. The noise was terrible.

'It was all fenced off with big signs up, "Danger – Keep Out", and searchlights and Alsatian dogs patrolling round it.

'Then Donna said something that really made me sit up. "Neville's gone out there tonight to look for the queens."

'"Oh my God," I thought, "I wonder if Charmaine knows? Doesn't she have enough on her plate, working day and night trying to keep her family in food and clothes without Neville getting stung, bitten or ending up in court?"

'"Well," I said to Donna, "he mustn't. It's too dangerous."

'"No," Donna says. "It's not too dangerous. Not from the wasps, it isn't. There was a lot more there in the summer."

'"What d'you mean?" I says.

'"Because of the rubbish," she said. "The wasps are all in the rubbish. They said on the TV that the wasps was in our mango, but they ain't. Our mango is clean. If you go down Ridley Market you see big piles of boxes and stuff – mouldy stuff – and the wasps go for that. They go for that rubbish. Then the dustmen come along, and it all goes off to the dump. It does, Aunty. It does."

'Well,' the woman said, 'suddenly it all clicked with me. I didn't know whether to laugh, or cry, or scream, or what. This little girl Donna had been sitting there all those weeks figuring it out all on her own. All summer, the wasps were settling on the empty fruit boxes down Ridley. The dustmen were lugging them off down to the dump, and hundreds and thousands of wasps were being rolled into the ground by them big rollers that squashed the rubbish. As like as not all that rolling kept it warm, as well. What a joke! They – the Council – had built a huge nest for the wasps, and here was little Donna telling me her brother Neville and his gang of mates was out there – right then and there – in the cold, and the dark, looking for the queens.

'Not that that bit was a joke, I must say. What if they did find the queens? They'd kill themselves trying to find them. What if they'd become giants living in the middle of that great warm heap of millions of layers of cardboard all covered in mouldy fruit and stuff. I didn't know who to turn to. I didn't want to call the police – they'd've picked up the kids for trespassing. I didn't want to tell Charmaine – not that I could, mind, at that moment, 'cos she was on the evening shift down the toy factory.

'"Switch that rubbish off, Donna," I said. "You seem to know more about it than all of them put together."

'They were busy showing pictures of someone in a gas mask in the basement of the sweet factory in Stoke Newington.

'"We're going out," I told her. "I'm following you," I said. "The hunt is on, love."

'So we went out – late and cold as it was – me and Donna. First thing we did was ring the Fire Brigade. I don't remember what I said I just remember screaming down the phone at those lads at the Fire Station.

'"There are some kids trapped out on the rubbish dump. I mean, if they aren't trapped now, then they very soon will be."

'Then I grabbed Donna and we made off for the dump. My heart was thumping away like nobody's business. When we got down there the rollers had stopped, 'cos the men had gone home. There was a light on in the night-watchman's hut, but no sign of the boys. I gave a shout through the fence.

'"Neville," I shouted. "Ne . . . ev."

'A voice came back – miles off – God knows where from.

'"Yeah – what you want?"

'"Come out of there, you'll get yourself killed," I said.

'At that, the nightwatchman came out with his dogs. It was the bloke all the kids called Dirty Dick. He was a strange feller. Everyone knew him, but no one knew where he came from. Besides he hated kids like Neville, and *they* hated him.

'"If I catch 'em, I'll kill 'em," he says, and he meant it, most like.

'Just then the Fire Brigade turns up, and there's little Donna crying her eyes out, holding on to my coat. A young feller jumps out of his fire engine, and he comes up to me.

'"Was it you, ma'am, that called the fire service?"

'"Yes," I say, "Yes, it was."

'"Where are these boys trapped?" he says.

'"Over there," I says, and I waved out across those great big heaps of rubbish. "They've got stuck looking for the queens."

'He looked at me as if I was barmy.

'"Looking for the Queen?" he says.

'"The queens – the queen wasps!" I says.

'"What – here?" he says.

'"Of course they're here," I said. "They're in the fruit boxes off of Ridley."

'He looked at me for a moment while it sunk in – and suddenly, it seemed to make sense to him, too.

'"Blimey," he said, just like that, very quiet. "Blimey!"

'He moved. Like greased lightning. It seemed like in a flash there was five, six of them in all the gear – masks, spray guns – the lot.

'"How do we get in here?" one of them was saying.

'I didn't know, and Dirty Dick had disappeared behind a heap of rubbish to kill Neville. But Donna knew. She shot out from behind me coat, and there she was twenty yards away, along the fence to where they'd used old doors when they'd run out of fencing wire – and, believe it or not – she just opened a door! They'd left one of the doors on its hinges, and the kids had made it their getting-in place. The firemen dashed off through the door.

'"Ne . . . ev," I screamed. "The firemen are coming in for you."'

The Bakerloo flea woman took in a breath.

'Yeah,' I said. 'So what happened to Neville?'

'Well the firemen found him with his mates, over by the River Lea, hacking away at some orange boxes. They hauled them out, and brought them back to me and Donna.'

'"Did you find 'em? Did you find the queens, Neville?" Donna shouted at him.

'Neville didn't answer.

'He wasn't saying. Neville and his mates weren't saying. No amount of me or the firemen – or Donna – going at them made them let on.'

The woman stopped, as if that was the end of the story.

'Well, what happened then,' I said.

'Well,' she said, 'Dirty Dick nailed up the door, and next day – you're not going to believe this – the very next day, that clown, the Minister of Wasps was down there, and for weeks and weeks after that, they were out there, behind that fence, behind the doors, drilling holes, spreading poisons and powders, and emptying gallons of stuff all over the dump.'

'But look, did they find the giant queen wasps?' I said. 'Did they?'

'Did they? Did they?' she says to me, and laughed.

'Look, did they find the giant queen wasps?' I said.

Then she laughed, and laughed and laughed.

'I tell you,' she said, 'they never found the giant queen

wasps and Donna never got a reward off of Tate and Lyle for saving their sugar for them.'

'So did they get rid of the winter wasps, then?' I asked.

'You seen any wasps about *this* winter?' she said.

'No,' I said. 'No, I can't say I have.'

'Well,' she said. 'They must have got rid of them, then, mustn't they?'

'Yeah,' I said, a bit doubtfully. 'They must have.'

'Funny old business, wasn't it?' she said.

'Yeah,' I said. 'Very funny.'

But I didn't laugh.

Lollipop lady

'Some people say roads aren't safe, don't they? But there was never anything wrong with roads. It's who or what goes along them that's wrong.'

You'll never guess who said that? It wasn't the Minister of Transport. It wasn't on the telly. It was my old friend the Bakerloo flea woman.

It happened like this. One evening a friend took me to their place for a chat and a late-night carry-out, and as we were all still chatting away after the last train, I stayed the night, sleeping across two armchairs. In the morning, when I left, it was after everyone else in the house had gone. I wasn't quite sure where I was, so when I came out of their house, I walked to the main road, and as I came round the corner, there was something that nearly took my eyes out.

Standing in front of me, by the side of a Belisha beacon and a zebra crossing was a lollipop woman. But the lollipop woman was not just any old lollipop woman, she was the Bakerloo flea lollipop woman. I was knocked sideways. I went up to her straight away.

'But it's you,' I said. 'It's you. I never knew you were a lollipop woman.'

'Neither did I,' she said.

'You know now though, don't you?' I said.

'No,' she said.

'Well, you've got the white coat, the blue hat and a STOP CHILDREN sign on the end of a pole. You look like a fair copy of one.'

'Good,' she said.

Every now and again she was having to stop me talking, because there'd be a school kid or two to take across the road.

"Why don't you know you're a lollipop woman?' I said.

'Sometimes things aren't quite as simple as they look,' she said.

'Why?' I asked.

'Look chum,' she said. 'Haven't you anything better to do than hang about on street corners asking a woman silly questions?'

'No,' I said.

'Fair enough,' she said. 'Give me ten minutes more of my duty here, and I'll meet you on the first bench on the left, through those gates over there, and I'll tell you the lot.'

So I went off into a bread shop, bought a hot chicken pie, went through the gate, turned left, and there was the bench. There was a pond with a duck on it, and two trees as well. The kind of place that gets called a park – in places where there aren't any parks. Then, ten minutes later, just as she said, she's there, in her white coat and blue hat and her STOP CHILDREN lollipop. She sat down beside me on the bench.

'Suits you,' I said, nodding at her coat.

'That's me battle-gear,' she said.

'Been out there fighting the juggernauts?' I asked.

'I'm not at war with *them*,' she said. 'They're only men doing a job.'

I knew by now, that if you want a story out of the Bakerloo flea woman, you have to keep pegging away and not get sidetracked. So I was a bit short.

'You're a lollipop woman,' I said. 'Why?'

She laughed a bit daft.

'Because a woman's got to do what a woman's got to do. Did you see that road out there?'

'The main road?' I said.

'No,' she said. 'The one that led onto it. That's what men in offices call a "through route". I know all the words now, you know. Two years ago the Johnson twins was killed on that through route, on their way to school. Last month a little boy – Otis Williams – was knocked down. Same time, same place. Both times, they tried to make out it was the kiddies' fault. They said they'd run out onto the road. Both times, they blamed the parents and teachers for not teaching the kids their crossing-the-road rules.'

'Who blamed them?' I asked.

'The papers. They said the kids weren't being looked after properly. Well, they hinted as much when they said their mothers was at work at the time.'

'I suppose it took those accidents for them to get around to putting up a zebra crossing out there.'

'Don't you believe it son,' she said. 'That's no real zebra crossing out there.'

'Like you're not a real lollipop woman?' I said.

'Right,' she says. 'You're learning. It was like this, see. For two years, after the death of those twins, the people in

these flats have said their kids aren't safe on this road. I tell
you, on the day of the funeral of the Johnson twins, almost
every single person on this estate turned out and blocked
the road for over an hour.

'I don't know how it started, but what I think happened
was that when the cars came to pick up the flowers and the
family, nearly everyone was out, lining the pavements to
show their respect. And when the coffins came out of the
flat it was just too much for many people, so the ones who
were on the wrong side of the road surged across the road
towards the car. Well, that fairly well blocked the road,
didn't it? And of course, it was not long before there were
cars and lorries coming along trying to get through to the
main road. Now those of us who were there, we weren't
having none of it. We were that upset, you know, it was
more than we could take. "You can wait," people were
saying. "Go round the other way."

'We shouted at them, and I remember, the feller driving the first truck stuck his head out of his cab, and shouted:

'"We can't get through on the other road. They've cut down the size of the road with pillars."

'That hit home. You see, he was talking about Websters Drive. And sure, if them up there didn't want no juggernauts, then all *they* needed to do was ring up the Council to put up a few pillars, and that's it. They don't call themselves "people" up there, they call themselves "residents", and it's "residents" who call the tune round here. Well, those pillars fairly made my blood boil. Just because the likes of us *drive* juggernauts doesn't mean we like juggernauts driving through our sitting room walls any more than "residents" do!

'So there we are in the middle of the road, holding up the traffic, paying our respects to the twins. The funeral cars went off, and we were left standing there, talking about things. Talking about the way the papers had had their sly dig at the twins' mother, and about the pillars. Any rate, somehow we just stayed there, waiting for the cars to come back from the cemetery.

'While we were waiting, some of the cars stuck in the jam started hooting, and their drivers got out and yelled at us, and kids ran about chanting, "You can't come through-oo, you can't come through-oo." I tell you, it was chaos. A policeman turned up, and went away. Two policemen turned up, and went away. But people just went on talking until the funeral cars came back.

'It was a bad day. Everyone knew the twins – like you always do know twins, don't you? – and with them both taken away in one fell swoop, it seemed awful. They'd come out between two cars, holding hands, just as this huge lorry was swerving to miss something coming at him. He had gone over the pair of 'em like they were paper dolls. The people who saw that are still having night-mares.

'After the day of the funeral, word went round that something had to be done about the traffic using our street as a short cut. All the more so now that Websters Drive was blocked off. Mrs Youngways, off the same balcony as the twins, started a petition. At the time, we thought it was a really good idea. We knocked up every single person on the estate, and down the street, to get them to sign the petition saying it had to stop. I can't remember the words but I think everyone signed it. Then we piled up all the signatures, and ten of us took it off to the Town Hall. We tried to get the local paper to take a picture of us on the steps handing it in. They didn't. So Vi Youngways sent a letter to them complaining, and the Editor said he thought we were using the twins' parents misfortunes to make political propaganda. Well, that really made us mad. No one had mentioned politics. All we wanted was a safe road.

'Anyway, we got a letter back off the Town Hall about how they'd look into it. I ask you, what was there to look into? A crystal ball? To tell us when the next one of our kids'd get killed – *and* blamed for it?

'Have you ever stood near to a heavy lorry as it rushes past you? The noise and the smell and the rush of air and the filth off it. The sheer weight of these things makes the ground shudder. What a thing for someone to send hurtling past people's bedrooms and front doors every day! Mad! Every time I see one now, I can see those twins.

'About a year later, we heard that "Nothing Could Be Done". The cars and lorries had to go on using our street. That's what the Council said, anyway.

'That was when it got to our ears that one of the people up the Town Hall who'd helped them come up with this Nothing Can Be Done business happened to live in Websters Drive. Websters Drive, with its fancy pillars and its "residents"! That bit of news went round the houses like wild fire. We were furious.

'Then, next thing, I saw a letter to the paper that said we needed a footbridge. Now, they're a right bind, they are. Anyway, why should you have to lug your shopping over them to dodge traffic that shouldn't be there in the first place? And there's always some nutter who'll drop off it, and some kids doing balancing acts on the hand rails.

'Just the suggestion got my blood up, but then, when someone else from the Council wrote and said we can't afford it, I was really mad. They were telling us our street wasn't worth the money, weren't they? And when I think of the money hanging about – especially up Websters Drive!

'Then it happened all over again. Otis Williams runs out onto the road, and some lunatic trying to get in to work quick, hits him. The boy flies into the air – the kiddie that saw him said he looked like a bonfire night guy all stuffed with straw – and he lands up on the roof of a car with a suntop. He didn't die poor lad – he did the next worst thing, 'cos he's been in a coma ever since.

'That was it for me. It was the last straw. I got up,

rushed out, and knocked up Vi Youngways. And we talked. We talked, and we talked. Everything had been done that could be done.

'"No," Vi said to me. "I've got a plan. There's going to be a zebra crossing across this road and a lollipop lady on it."

'I groaned.

'"Look Vi, you must be joking. Do you think that that crowd, up there at the Town Hall, are going to lay aside the money for that, when they say there isn't the money to replace the kids' seesaw, or pay someone to sweep the broken glass off the playground?"

'"We're not going to *ask* them," Vi said. "We're going to do it ourselves – and ask later! All we've got to do is find some white paint for the road, a white mac and paint up a lollipop and we're laughing."

'"Oh yes," I said, "and pop down the ironmongers, and buy a couple of Belisha beacons on the never-never. Easy! You're crazy, Vi!"

'"Yes," she said, "I am. But we'll do it – bit by bit – because it has to be done. First thing we do is go and look at a crossing, and make a list of everything we need. I can't even remember what it actually says on the lollipop. What does it say?"

'Well, Vi's kids was coming in from school just then, and as they came rushing in through the door with their mates – to grab a biscuit and switch on the telly – she yells at them.

'"No telly for you lot tonight. You've got homework to do."

'"We ain't got none," they say.

"'Oh yes, you have," she says. "You've got *my* home-work to do. I've got a quiz for you."

"'A quiz?" they go. "A quiz? No, come on Mum, don't be daft."

'In the end she got them all pinned down in the front room – even those that aren't hers.

"'Right, how many stripes are there on a zebra cross-ing?"

"'Twelve," one of them shouts.

"'Six" another says.

"'As many as you need to fill the road," Darren says.

"'How wide is a stripe on a zebra crossing?"

'They all go quiet.

"'Pass," Ibby says, and we all laugh.

"'Right," Vi says. "How high is a Belisha beacon?"

"'A what?"

"'It's the orange lights, you berk," Darren says.

"'Ask us real questions, like football."

"'How high is a Belisha beacon?" Vi says.

"'How high, Mum?"

"'*I* don't know," Vi says. "I'm asking *you*."

"'Haven't you got the answers there, then?"

"'No, I'm trying to find out. Look," she says. "We want to know all the facts about zebra crossings."

"'How do you expect us to know all of them?"

"'Well, you're always out on the streets, aren't you?" Vi says.

'The other kids – not hers – are trying to get out the door again. They think she's going crazy. So I have a go then.

"'Look," I says. "This is no game. You know Otis, you

remember the Johnson twins? Right, well, Vi's got this plan. We're going to paint our own zebra crossing on the road. And we're . . ."

"'We could do it all different colours," says one of them. "Doesn't have to be black and white, does it?"

"'Course it does," Vi says. "And the other thing we've got to make is a lollipop. Who can remember what's written on that?"

"'It says, STOP!"

"'No it don't. It says, CROSS NOW."

"'I know where you can nick one," someone goes.

"'We're nicking nothing," Vi says.

"'You know the women's hats are different from the men's," Lorraine says.

"'Right, we've got to find out all these things," Vi says, and she looks at me, Vi does and winks.

"'I saw you," Darren says. "What you going to do?"

'So now, Vi shuts the door on the six kids there.

"'Right," she says. "What I'm going to say now is so secret that we're going to have to swear solemnly and forever never to tell anyone. Because if anyone tells, all hell will be let loose on them."

'The way Vi said that, it scared *me*.

"'I want to go home now," Patrick says, one of her kids' friends.

"'Too late," Vi says.

'I thought that was a bit much. Poor kid looked scared stiff.

'Vi shut the curtains. She really meant business now. Then she turned to us all, and says what was on her mind.

"'We've all got to swear together, never, never, never

to tell anyone about what we're going to do. Because if anyone finds out, before we do it, they'll try and stop us."

'I couldn't hold myself back.

'"Well, when are we going to do it?" I said.

'"Tonight," Vi said. "No point in hanging about. We've been hanging about for two years, and a fat lot of good that's done us. We're going to go out onto the road at three o'clock in the middle of the night, and paint that zebra crossing on the road. Then we're going to rig up two beacons and come the morning, we're going to have a lollipop man on the crossing."

'I thought Vi had gone off her rocker.

'"You're crazy, girl." I said. "You're crazy! These children can't stay up all hours painting stuff on roads."

'"Course they're not," Vi says. "I'm only asking them to keep a secret till the morning."

'Then she looks round the room till she sees a very old picture on top of the telly – a photo in a frame – of a man with an enormous beard.

'"That man," she says, "was my grandfather. He was a terrible feller. Outside the house, everyone thought he was a great man. But indoors he was like thunder and lightning. A truly terrible man."

'She got the picture down off the telly.

'"Right," she says. "We're all going to swear in front of old grandad to keep our secret about tonight. Ready? Altogether, say after me, WE SWEAR . . ."

'"We swear."

'"TO KEEP THE SECRET."

'"To keep the secret."

'"NEVER TO TELL."

'"Never to tell."

'"CROSS MY HEART."

'"Cross my heart."

'"HOPE TO DIE."

'"Hope to die."

'"HEAR US NOW."

'"Hear us now."

'"GRANDAD."

'"Grandad."

'You could almost see the old feller in the photograph frown, as if to say: And you'd better mean it.

'"Right," Vi says. "To work. We've got a lot to do. Who's going to go out and measure up a zebra crossing?"

'"Me," Darren says.

'"Me," Lorraine says.

'"Right," Vi says, giving Darren the tape measure. "Everything, measure everything."

'"Now who's left? Ibby, John, Sarah, and you and me, girl. What are we going to need?"

'"Paint."

'"Who's got paint?"

'Well, two doors down from me I knew was George and his son and they were sign painters. If I could rope them in, we'd be laughing.

'"How about the orange beacons?" Ibby said. "How can we do *them*?"

'"I know," Vi says. "Woollies do a line in plastic lampshades that look like a goldfish bowl. John, Ibby, you've just got time. Nip up to Woollies on your bikes and buy two. Here's a fiver. Now what else?"

'We counted up. A white coat. Two poles. One broomstick. And that's when we ran into trouble. It was easy to work out how to turn the broomstick into a lollipop. But we couldn't think how to make the beacon poles.

'Well, it was at that point I thought things weren't quite right. It was all very well us getting the kids to keep a secret, but what we should've been doing, rightly, was doing this with everyone in the know. So I said as much to Vi.

'"We've got to draw *everyone* in on this, and not be doing it like a bank raid," I said.

'"Oh yes," Vi said. "And all the old windbags'll sit there saying as how it can't be done."

'"Vi," I said. "You're wrong."

'I looked at her clock. Five-thirty.

'"By half seven, we'll have fifty people in the laundry

over this. Quick," I said to one of the kids. "Give us your felt tips, and your scrapbook."

'I wrote on it in big letters.

NO MORE DEATHS
MEETING 7.30
LAUNDRY
TONIGHT

'Sarah knew straight away what to do. "I can go round the flats with it like a poster telling people to come," she said.

'"Right, on your way," I said.

'After that, I went out, and Vi waited in for the kids to come back with the gear and the facts. Then we all went round the flats, knocking up friends, and friends of friends asking them had they heard.

'So come seven-thirty, there was quite a crowd down there at the laundry. I gave Vi a push, and she really gave it to them. Great, she was.

'"Look," she says. "You remember the Johnson twins, and the Williams' boy who's still in a coma? Well, we've got to do something fast, and I've got a plan. Tonight we could make a zebra crossing across Jifford Street, and we'll have a lollipop lady on it in time to take the kids across in the morning. So, what do you think?"

'At that, there was uproar. Everyone began talking at once. Some people were laughing, some people were saying, "It's against the law", and others were saying, "I'd go to prison if it means saving kids' lives".

'"Now, come on everyone," I said. "Let's be practical. Right, Darren, read out what you've got there."

'He told everyone what they'd found out, and then Vi held up a broomstick and Ibby and John held up two plastic lampshades and Sarah holds up a white coat she'd got from the chip-shop lady, and George, the sign painter, held up the paint.

'"And that's as far as we've got," Vi says.

'Everyone cheered like mad.

'"But what are we going to do about the poles for the beacons?" George asked.

'Darren was right in there with the facts about how fat they are. But, for a moment, we couldn't crack it – until Lorraine remembered something they'd done at school. "Couldn't we build them out of old Vim and Ajax cans. We once did that at school, once," she said.

'Everyone cheered like mad, and people rushed off to get old Vim cans. George the sign painter talked to the kids about what it says on the lollipop, so he could get on with that right away. A couple of men there were arguing about what paint was best, and they had at least half a dozen kids dancing round them saying, "Can we come, can we do some?"

'They were dying to stay out until three in the morning and splash a bit of paint on the road. To tell the truth I was, too. The idea of taking hold of a great big paint brush and sloshing a great white stripe across the road in the dead of night appealed to me, too.

'"This is better than all your secret service stuff with grandad, isn't it?" I said to Vi.

'"So long as no one goes and tells The Law on us," she says.

'After a while, people drifted off to bed, and there was

only a few of us left to actually do the deed, and we're sitting there in the laundry in the middle of the night with the paint and the brushes, and the old Vim cans when, suddenly, Ibby looks up and asks the question we'd all forgotten to ask.

'"So who's going to be the lollipop lady?"

'There was total silence, and because no one else spoke up – I did.

'"I will, I'll be your actual lollipop lady – and I'll need a hat for the job," I said.

'I picked up a peaked hat that was lying there.

'"How do I look?" I said.

'"Not a flat cap," Lorraine said. "Lollipop women wear higher ones."

'"Well, we can't get one of them now."

'Then Ibby said, "Saliq could make one."

'"Could he?" Vi says.

'"Course," he says.

'"Will you ask him, then?" Vi says.

'And off went Ibby.

'About two hours later, at gone midnight, Ibby came over to the laundry with Saliq. Saliq took out a bag, and wrapped in tissue paper was a navy-coloured hat with a peak. On the front there was a little silver badge that said Somebody-or-others' Cricket Club. It looked marvellous.'

As I sat there with the Bakerloo flea woman, I looked at the hat, and there the badge was.

'Yes,' she said, 'that was it. We were all set. So we waited until three in the morning – a little band of us. There was me, George the painter, and two of his pals with brushes and rollers, a couple of young lads who said they'd rig the beacons up with staples and superglue and buckets. And there was two girls who said they'd keep look-out on the two corners for panda cars.

'We crept out onto the road, and the funny thing was, I wasn't scared. I had the feeling that, in every one of the flats, there was someone peeping from behind the curtains wishing us well. Oh it was lovely. It went like a well-oiled machine. No one spoke out loud. We just got on with the job, out there in the middle of the road, in the dead of night. I've never seen paint look so white. And the beacons – they looked a treat.

'Everything went smoothly until one of the guards came running around the corner.

'"Scarper," she says. "Scarper."

'"Who is it?" I says.

'"Feller with a dog."

'"Who?"

'"I don't know," she says.

'"OK," I said to the others. "Leave the beacons here, pick up your gear, and we'll wait down the alley."

'They grabbed their paint and roller, and we made off for the alley. We had a view from where we were, and saw the man they call the Major come round the corner with his dog. It couldn't have been worse, because he's the kind of bloke who prides himself on spotting something funny or suspicious going on, ringing for the law, and getting himself a medal for it.

'We held our breath. Him and his dog get to our brand new, half finished zebra crossing, and – he didn't notice anything. His dog did, though. It only goes up to our

lovely new Belisha beacon, sniffs it, sticks its leg up and baptizes it, doesn't it? But the Major, he didn't bat an eyelid. We crouched there in the alley waiting for him to twig, but the dog finishes, and he carries on up the road. If he had cottoned on to what was going on, I'm sure as sure can be, he'd've been on the hot line to his pals up at the police station. He's that desperate for a knighthood.

'When he'd gone, we came running out of the alley and the painters finished off. I had a go, too. I did one of them zig-zags. It was a lovely feeling spreading this white paint on the road. It felt like naughty – but right – all at the same time. You felt proud, but wicked. I can look at that bit of the zig-zags on the crossing now, and say – "I did that bit." I suppose all the others do the same with their bits.

'Anyway, job done, we packed up, and dashed back to my place for a quick cup and a sandwich. There *were* people looking out their windows, dotted about all over the block. I could see faces looking out at us as we crossed the courtyard. Waving and laughing, so we waved back. You'd've thought we'd won the cup or something. Mind you, that's what it felt like.

'Back at my place there was a welcoming party, quiet but excited, all giggles and whispers. The Major's dog got the biggest laugh of the night. Anyway most of us had work to go to in two or three hours' time – not least me – in Eva's white coat, and Saliq's hat.

'"Come on, girl, let's be having you. Let's see you in your gear," someone says.

'So I put on my chip-shop overall, and picked up my lollipop, and someone pinned on my hat, and I stand there. Then one of the lads does the Duke of Edinburgh on me. He puts his hands behind his back, and does the walk past. Inspection job. He walks past me, stops, comes back, and speaks.

'"Very good. Very good. One of our old lollipop girls – very good."

'Suddenly he looks at my hat.

'"Cricket Club? Cricket Club? What are you? Bowler?"

'I curtsey.

'"No your Majesty," I say. "I'm bats."

'Everyone laughed, and we all went "Sh . . . sh . . . sh", and we fell into the armchairs laughing, and trying to keep quiet.

'Two hours later, there's me on the road stopping my first lorry. Everyone was coming past laughing and wishing me good luck, and when I stopped that first one, there were people in the flats all looking out of their windows, calling down to me, and clapping and whistling and cheering. You'd have thought I was a footballer or something the carry-on there was, and every now and then, I looked up and saw those Woollies lampshades sitting on top of the poles, and I could hardly stop myself from laughing.

'Still, I must have taken more than a hundred kiddies safely across the road, on the way to school, and a hundred back, at going home time. I thought the papers'd be down, or the telly, but maybe they're afraid that if they show us doing it, others'll get the same idea. Then where would they be?'

'Have the police been down and stopped you?' I asked.

'Not yet,' she said. 'This is only my second morning on.

For all I know, the Council'll bring round their wall cleaning mob, and scrub the road clean.'

'What will you do then?' I asked.

'Paint it again.'

'You could be put away for holding up traffic and wearing a uniform.'

'Well then, Vi'd come and do it.'

'And then, Vi'd get done,' I said.

'Well then, Otis's mother'd do it.'

'Would she?' I said.

'Of course,' the Bakerloo flea woman said. 'Anyway, we'll keep going and in the end they'll have to make it lawful. They'll have to. And I'll tell you something else. Once it's lawful, they'll have to find the funds to pay for it.'

And that was that. She didn't have anything else to say to me and I couldn't think of anything else to ask her.

'I'm parched after my morning stint, I'm off home to grab a quick cup of tea,' she said, and was up and off down the road in her white coat, blue hat, and carrying her lollipop with her.

Amazing sight it was. Amazing woman, isn't she?

The loaf and the knife

I was on the last bus going down Willesden Lane one Wednesday night. I was going to stay with a friend that way. I was upstairs looking down on the street below, when I heard this awful coughing. So I looked round and it was the Bakerloo flea woman – the woman who knew all about those wasps, and all that.

'I don't believe it,' I said.

'Hallo,' she said. 'Can't keep out of each other's way, can we? It's becoming a habit, isn't it?'

'Don't like your cough,' I said.

'Do you think I do?' she said.

'I suppose not,' I said.

'It's not as if it's the only thing I'm bothered by.' She said.

'Don't tell me,' I said. 'You've got a . . . er . . . a plague of something – slugs. Giant slugs in your bath.'

'Don't be funny,' she says.

'I'm sorry.'

She didn't say anything, so I asked her myself.

'Well, what's bothering you?' I said.

'Oh, it's only a little thing.'

'Yeah?' I said, not believing her.

'Well, I'm not superstitious,' she said. 'I don't believe in any of these things like horoscopes or fortune-telling. None of it.'

'Neither do I,' I said.

'But I used to have mice in my house.'

'Don't we all?' I said.

'I don't any more,' she said.

'Lucky you,' I said.

'Not a bit of it. I'd give anything in the world to have one or two of the little devils back, if I could.'

'You *want* mice? You actually want mice? Look,' I said. 'I can do you a favour, any time. I've never really said "thank you" for telling me those stories.'

'They weren't stories,' she said.

'No, no, of course not,' I said. 'But if you want a couple of mice, don't worry, I can get some for you. A friend of mine works in a laboratory – a medical friend. They're chopping them up all hours of the day and night to try and find a cure for cancer or something.'

'Don't, don't, don't,' she says. 'Don't tell me. I can't stand it.'

Funny, I thought. There's this woman who's scared the wits out of me telling me about giant wasps and giant fleas, and here she is getting jumpy about a few mice. Something very strange must have happened to her. I didn't say that to her though. Instead I said:

'So you don't want any new mice then?'

'Wouldn't make any difference to me now. It's too late.'

'Too late for what?'

'The picture in my eye. You can't wipe that out.'

'Wipe what out?'

The woman looked as if she was in a dream, but she went on talking.

'And it's not as if that old lady didn't warn me, either.

She said she'd do it so long as I promised I wouldn't watch her while she was doing it. But I couldn't stop myself. I had to. You know how it is. Someone says to you, you can have what you like so long as you keep your eyes shut. You shut your eyes, you wait, and before you know you've done it, you're peeping. Oh dear, it happened to me, and I wished to God it never had. And she warned me, mind.

'"I'll do it for you, girl," she said. "But whatever you do, don't watch me, or you'll be cursed by the picture of it in your mind till your dying day." And she was right.'

'Who?' I said. 'Who are you talking about? What happened?'

'Oh it was nothing, really,' she said.

'Oh come on,' I said. 'You can't just leave it like that.'

'I warn you,' she said. 'You're a fool to ask.'

'Why?' I said.

'Because it'll live in your eye like it's lived in mine.'

'I'll risk it,' I said.

'I used to suffer from mice,' she told me. 'I'm not scared of them like some folks are. I don't mind looking at them. I don't mind seeing them. It's the ones I don't see that worry me. I hate the thought of them running along under the boards, looking out at you through the cracks in the walls, making their nests in corners under cupboards, but worst of all, I hate getting up in the morning, and finding their little doings on top of the fridge. So I lay traps – ordinary traps – the ones that snap shut so hard they could break your finger while you're setting them. I used to put little bits of broken Kit-Kat on them. Funny that, I always think, funny that mice love something called Kit-Kat.

'The trouble with traps, though, is that you're only

catching them one at a time, aren't you? Well, in the time it takes to catch one, they've had eight babies, haven't they? And anyway, I can never be sure that leaving bits of Kit-Kat about doesn't attract them. All the others that came for a bit don't get caught, do they?'

'No,' I said.

'So, I got the rat-catcher in. He put little cake trays all around full of what looked like sawdust and wood shavings. He was a very nice young man, I thought, much too nice to be bothering himself all day long with how to kill mice and rats and bedbugs and things. I gave him a cup of tea, and as he drank his tea, I could not help looking at his hands. I thought of all the horrible places they must have been, and all the horrible creatures he must have handled.'

'Like what?' I said.

'Lice,' she said. 'Dead lice.

'Anyway, he left the little trays.

'"The mice'll eat this poison," he said. "And they'll just keel over and die until the whole lot cop it."

'"Where?" I say to him.

'"Well," he says, "wherever they are going about their business."

'"You mean I'm going to have dead mice all over the place, dying under my floorboards, or in the middle of the kitchen floor?"

'"Oh no," he says. "This stuff burns them up. You won't get no smell, neither. Like I said, they gobble it up, keel over, then the stuff – the poison, like – it burns them up from the inside."

'Well, I don't know if he has better luck elsewhere, or

what, but my mice weren't fooled. They must have taken one look at them little trays and said to each other, "Trouble! Don't touch it, none of you! It may look juicy but really it's poison."

'He was a nice enough fellow, that rat-catcher. It's just that I had especially clever mice. You see what I've learnt is that it's no use treating mice like you would bugs and flies. They've got ways of telling each other what's going on. They stick together, and this is what makes them hard to beat.'

'So how did you get rid of them then?' I said to the Bakerloo flea woman. 'Look, come on, tell me, if you're going to tell me. If not, forget it.'

'Don't push it, son,' she says. 'I'll tell you if you really want me to. But I'm warning you! What I tell you might live in your head for the rest of your days, like it has in mine.'

'Right, I'm ready for anything you've got for me,' I said.

'Well, everyone round our way knows Mrs Kent. And, if they don't know *her*, they know *of* her. She's lived there all her life, and all her people before her. Someone said to me, if you got mice, go see Mrs Kent, she'll fix them for you. So, because all else had failed, that's what I done.

'Now, everyone knows it's never much use knocking up Mrs Kent, because she's hardly ever in, and when she's in, she's asleep. You have to wait to catch her on the street. So one day, not long after my superman and his little trays had come, and I was finding their trails of doings on my draining board, I saw old Mrs Kent coming down the road. I started in on her direct.

"'Hallo dear – you got a way with mice have you, Mrs Kent?"

"'So what if I have?" she says.

"'If you have," I say, "would you be feeling like doing someone a favour?"

"'I might – but then I might not. What's your trouble?"

"'I got mice," I say.

"'What's so wrong with that?" she said.

"'I don't want them," I said. "I don't like their dirt."

"'They're no dirtier than the houses they're living in," she said.

"'Well, my house is clean," I said.

"'Well, so are your mice," she says.

"'Well, I don't want them eating my food," I say.

"'What, can't you afford it?" she says.

'Now I'm getting a bit hot under the collar about this – but, I stood my ground.

'"I like to choose who I sit down and eat with – put it like that."

'"You had the Council in, have you?"

'"Yes," I said.

'"Did it take?" she said.

'"Did what take?" I said.

'"Did the poison take?"

'"No," I said. "They didn't take it."

'"Then you've got the bad 'uns," she said. "You've got the bad 'uns. They're mad that lot."

'Well, between you and me, I thought there was only one of us standing there who was mad and it weren't me. But I wasn't saying anything. She did though.

'"Right I'll do it for you," she said, muttering away to herself, like she's really got it in for these mice. "I know this lot. Never mind your experts, I'll get rid of these here mice of yours, but I'm warning you, don't you watch me doing it. That's all I ask of you. No money. Nothing. Just don't watch me doing it, or what you see will live with you for the rest of your life. You promise?"

'"I promise," I said.

'"I'll come to you," she says, "as soon as I can."

'A couple of days later, half eleven at night, I'm just unplugging my telly, going off to bed when a knock comes at the door. It's her.

'"I've come to get 'em," she says, and she's over my step and in – without a by-your-leave, or nothing.

'"Got a knife?" she says, getting to the kitchen before I do.

'"Yes," I say, showing her my drawer.

'"Steel, the lot of them," she says. "Stainless steel. That's no good. Ain't you got no iron knives?"

'Last time I saw an iron knife was my old nan's, and *she* must have had that since before the first war.

'"I like to use the knife of the house," she says. "But I've got me own."

'Then she stopped and pointed her finger directly at me.

'"This is where you go, girl. Leave me to me business. But mark my words, don't watch me at my business."'

Now, remember, I was on this bus late at night, and here was the Bakerloo flea woman telling me the story of this other woman and when she said 'Mrs Kent pointed her finger at me', the Bakerloo flea woman pointed *her* finger at *me*. It was as if the woman I did *not* know was pointing her finger at me through the arm and finger of the woman I *did* know.

'I shut the door leaving her my kitchen,' she told me. 'But something drew me back to that door. I turned, got down on my knees – and there I was, like some Peeping Tom, peering through the keyhole.

'First thing she does is sit down at my table, take her bag on to her lap, and out of her bag she takes half a loaf of bread. Next, she takes a little penknife. Now, this little penknife had two rusty blades – one either end. The one she sticks in the open end of the loaf where it's sawn off, and the other she just opens it out, blade up.

'Next thing, she takes up the loaf with the knife stuck in it, and she starts off around the room as if she's looking for one of these mice. In the end, she comes to a hole, between the boards and the skirting, and straightway, she's laying down the loaf, a little way back from the hole, with the open blade of the knife sticking out. Next thing, she takes my chair and sets it down a little way back from the loaf and knife. Then, she switched out the light, and she went and sat on the chair. Only the lights from the street shone in. And there she sat, staring at the loaf and knife, and beyond it, to the hole in the wall. And there was me, peering through the keyhole, not daring to breathe.

'She sat there, staring at that hole for what seemed like a lifetime, until – all of a sudden – there was a little sound. Scrape, scrape, and out of the hole came a mouse. It came, slow, careful, sniffing up to the blade of the knife. Mrs Kent sat there with the street lights shining in, her eyes fixed, not a hair of her moving. And there was me at the keyhole staring.

'The mouse stopped at the blade, sniffed again, then – back it ran to the hole. And still she sat, and still she stared, until all of a sudden, there was another little sound. Scrape, scrape, and out of the hole came a mouse. Maybe it was the same one, maybe it was its next-door neighbour. I shall never know. I couldn't see clear enough, anyhow. Anyways, this time it came careful, sniffing its way up to the blade, and when it got to the blade, it ran its whiskers along the length of the blade. It stopped for a moment, and then in a flash, it was back down the hole.

'Still she sat. Still she stared. And there I was still outside the door, scarcely daring to breathe, my eye stuck to that keyhole. Then, all of a sudden, for a third time, comes a mouse. Maybe the same mouse, maybe a third, maybe the one she was really after, but this time it was different. This time it came as if its back legs were holding it back. They were fighting to stay put, but its front legs was pulling, pulling, pulling it on. There was a real struggle going on inside that mouse, and the whole time it was making this mouse noise. The squeak, squeak, squeak you hear under your floorboards at night.

'So this mouse, coming faster than it was going, digging its back legs in, with its front legs pulling, got to the blade. And this you'll never believe. It got to the blade. It put its head over the blade, and in one stroke, it ran its neck along the length of the blade, and slit its little throat – until it moved no more. The blood ran from out of its neck, and its body lay still on the floor.

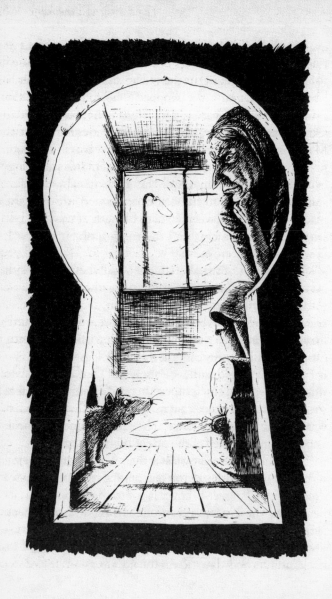

'At that, old Mrs Kent, she got up, she took a cloth and a paper bag out of her bag, and she picked the mouse up by its tail, and put it in the paper bag. She put the paper bag back into her bag, she mopped the blood off the floor, wiped her knife clean, put the cloth in her bag, pulled the knife out of the loaf, snapped the blades shut, put the knife in the bag, and put the loaf in the bag.

'And the whole time it went on, I was still watching. I just could not tear myself away from that keyhole. She got up, turned, and came towards the door. And still I could not tear myself away. She opens the door, and there I am, still on my knees.

'"Don't say I never told you," she said. "I warned you. What you've just seen will live in your head till your dying day. It'll torment you for the rest of your life, or till you find a way of ridding yourself of it."'

At that the woman, the Bakerloo flea woman, turned on me sitting there upstairs on the last bus home with a funny look in her eye.

'And I have, I just have!' she said. 'I feel easy in myself for the first time since I seen the whole business with the loaf and knife because I've just told *you* all that happened.'

She pointed again, right at me, and laughed, her face relaxed. She looked out of the window of the bus.

'Good lord,' she says. 'My stop.'

She slipped away off the bus, taking a quick last look at me.

'Now it'll live with *you* for the rest of *your* life, and torment *you* like it did *me*, till *you* find a way to get rid of it.'

And that was that. She left me there, four or five stops

past my stop on the last bus. I had to walk back, over a mile, through the dark streets, thinking about what she said.

'It'll live with you for the rest of your life, and torment you like it did me, till you find a way to get rid of it.'

And I found myself saying, How? How can *I* get rid of it?

Custard's last stand

I like big hamburgers. There are all different kinds of burgers you can get, aren't there? MacDonalds, Wimpys, Caseys, Wendyburgers, Sizzles. We've got one round our way. I've forgotten what it's called – Biggyburgers or something. I was sitting in there the other day at the window, just by the bus stop, and there, outside, standing in the queue was the Bakerloo flea woman. I banged on the window. Everyone seemed to look round except her. I pointed at her to make the man next to her tell her that someone wanted her. She turned, saw me and waved. I waved and went back to my Biggyburger and was busy munching away when suddenly there she was.

'I might just as well wait for that bus in here,' she says. 'How are you keeping, old son?'

'I'm fine,' I said, 'fine. How about yourself?'

'Nothing to complain of,' she said. 'I've got the dodgy knee, mind, but there you go, you can't win 'em all, can you? What's that you're eating?' she said.

'A Biggyburger or something,' I said.

'You eat them, do you?' she said.

'Sure I do. I love them.'

'Huh, you wouldn't if you knew what was in them,' she says.

'What are you talking about? It says here "One hundred per cent beef". Beef, right?'

'Oh well, if that's what it says, you got to believe them, haven't you?' she said. Then she laughed.

'Now hold it,' I said. 'What are you telling me?'

'No, no. Nothing, love. For all I know, *your* beefburger *is* one hundred per cent beef.'

'Thank you,' I said.

'On the other hand, for all I know it's something else,' she said.

'Like what?'

'Horse, donkey, kangaroo . . .'

'You what?' I said.

'No, I'm not saying *your* beefburger is.'

'What *are* you saying then?' I said.

'Well, I used to work in one of these here places, you know.' she says.

'When was this?' I said.

'Oh, years ago now,' she said, 'before Macdonalds, before Wimpys even. This is years ago. There was a feller in the West End who opened up a place called the Yum Yum Burger Bar. He had it all decked out like a kind of Wild West Saloon, with "Wanted" posters all over the walls. Pictures of old-time cowboys like Wyatt Earp and Buffalo Bill and John Wayne were stuck up all over the shop.

'I didn't mind that so much, but *we* all had to get up in Wild West outfits an' all. People on the till, the cooks, the washers-up, even the cleaners, would you believe? I think some of the *fellers* actually liked it, swaggering about with toy pistols by their side, thinking they were off for a shoot-out every time they emptied the rubbish bins.'

'What were you wearing, then?' I said.

'Oh, me. Well, I told 'em I wasn't wearing one of them silly gingham frock things, so they said I could be a stable girl. I just wore khaki shirt and trousers. Oh yeah – and blessed boots. I felt like I was in the Women's Army most of the time.'

'What was the food like?' I said.

'Oh, the food. Now you're talking. Well, you could have the Yum Yum Burger, the Yum Yum Rodeo, the Yum Yum Rancher or the Yum Yum Round-up. Can you imagine? Grown people coming in off the streets of London, going up to some young lad from Dagenham or somewhere – who just so happens to be dolled up in a white stetson hat – and saying, "I'll have a Yum Yum Round-up, please." Ridiculous.

'And he had names for all the sauces and stuff. There was the Texas Tangee, Monument Valley Mix and Colorado Crispee. In actual fact they were all made in Manchester by the manager's brother-in-law.'

'What kind of man was this manager, then?' I said.

'Oh, the manager. Him. His main trouble was his shirts was all too small. He had this pot belly in front of him, and he was forever bursting out of it all over the shop. He came from Romford but we used to call him General Custer – or General Custard. No, the man was a villain.

'The place was a giant success, mind. He had John Wayne flown over specially to open it. It was Britain's first Burger Bar. For the first few months, the place was packed. He was open all hours, so some of us was working twelve, even sixteen hours a day. By the end of the day your feet felt like a steam roller had run over them – and, lord, your back. Of course he'd get young fellers wanting to work there who thought it was kind of glamorous to be selling Yum Yum Rodeos next to Leicester Square Station.

'He paid us under the rate because we had free meals. Yum Yum meals, morning, noon and night.

'Mind, you didn't get any more money if you *didn't* have a Yum Yum meal. Now, this was going on fourteen hours a day, six days a week: Yum Yum Burgers, breakfast, dinner, tea, supper. Something was bound to crack, wasn't it? I mean Saturday nights you'd get invaded with people shouting and pushing. The heat in there was like Kew Gardens.

'I remember one time this drunk American coming in and he thought all the lads in their stetsons and gun-belts were taking the mickey out of him.

'"Say kid," he was yelling, "you take that ten-gallon hat off or I'll push you through that wall."

'One of the fellers, Titch – and he *was* small – was there going, "What? What?"

'And the American stands up. He's about two foot taller than Titch and he grabs Titch's stetson and tries to lift it off his head, but it's tied under Titch's chin. He tugs it and nearly yanks Titch's head off. This sends Titch spare. Next minute, his fists are flailing against the American's belly.

'I don't know whether it was out of shock or whether it was where Titch caught him, but then this American is sick. All over Titch. Fair and square. Oh, my goodness, it was awful. Worse than a fight. There's people jumping up, rushing out, people screaming. The huge American standing there in his check shirt, looking at the mess –

and Titch, poor feller. I think he could have taken a slap round the chops, a punch in the eye, anything, except that. All over him. He just cried out of rage.

'Anyway, we pushed the American feller out of the shop, but of course there was nowhere out the back for Titch to wash down or nothing. He went and hid in the toilet for the next two hours. He went home in an old overall with his hairy legs sticking out the bottom. I suppose the only good thing to come of it was knowing that Custard'd have to buy Titch a new cowboy outfit.

'It was about this time, some strange things started happening. One after another, we all went down with awful stomach pains. It was during a heatwave. If people thought when they came into Yum Yum's they was coming deep into the heart of Texas, they could believe it. It was unbearable. And these stomach aches. You've never had pain like this, son. It felt like you'd swallowed a hedgehog. You didn't dare move, breathe or talk, for fear that that hedgehog'd go walking round your guts.

'We was all getting it. And you see we couldn't take time off or nothing because Custard used to threaten us with the sack. So we were coming in to work, serving Yum Yum Round-ups or whatever in agony, complete agony. All this with the heat as well. You imagine, General Custard, he used to tell us we had to look all cheery, so that when somebody said they wanted a Yum Yum Rodeo or something, we were to smile at them and say things like, "Monument Valley Mix goes well with that, sir," and then we were to say, "Apple Shoot-out to follow, sir? Cowhand Coffee?" and all that, to try and make them spend more money, you see. But you try and do all that with a hedgehog going through your insides, and the temperature in the nineties.

'Just even to *look* at one of those Yum Yum Burgers frying on the hot-plate was enough to turn your innards over. And you'd look up and you'd see rows and rows of people all biting into their Yum Yums with sauce dribbling down their chins. The mood in the place was awful. People serving up the stuff and rushing out the back for a you-know-what. It got to all of us. Except Custard. He seemed fine.

'And you know, when you work in kitchens, in the heat, and in cramped conditions, you don't wear much, and you're always brushing past each other. It's like you're all working in a steam bath, a sauna or something. But when we came down with this gut-rot you couldn't bear for anyone to come anywhere near you. Your skin felt like it could only just hold in your flesh. The flesh was trying to get out through the pores of your skin.

'I remember once, I was on kitchen duty, and I was standing there with the pains going from front to back, top to bottom. The sweat was pouring off me, and Rosetta walked in with a pile of raw Yum Yums and dumped them down next to the hot-plate. I don't know what it was, but at that moment, it was like I heard a voice in my ear that said, "Them Yum Yums are dodgy." I don't know what it was. Maybe it was the first time I'd ever seen them all together in a big heap like that because normally I was out the front doing the tables. So, as I had a second, and as people weren't shouting for me to fetch, carry, wash and wipe, I went over and looked at this great pile of raw Yum Yums.

'I don't know whether you know, but meat goes brown when it gets old. And it gets kind of dry and shrunk. Well, these Yum Yums looked like bits of mouldy cardboard. And then I took a whiff of them. It wasn't a particularly strong smell, but when you got in close and really stuck your nose in there, it smelt like the inside of a broken fridge full of food. Repulsive.

'So, of course, I got to thinking about all this. Could the famous, the great, the fabulous Yum Yum Burgers be giving us this awful gut-ache? At first I thought no, because the thousands of people coming in to the Yum Yum Burger Bar would all have gone down with it, wouldn't they? Then again, I thought, most of the people that come into Yum Yum's were one-offs: they were people passing through. (You know, they'd seen John Wayne on telly opening the place and so they had promised their kids a visit there when they next came to London.) Maybe just *one* Yum Yum wasn't enough to give you the collywobbles, or the "hedgehogs" as I was calling them by now.

'Then the awful Grace business happened. Grace was a dear old soul. She was one of those old dears who walk round the place with all they own in polythene bags. She didn't have anywhere to live. In summer she slept in shop doorways – stuffed newspaper up her jumper, got into a cardboard box and dozed off like that. She used to feed the birds in the park. The kids told me that she used to put bread on her lips and the birds'd come and peck the bread out of her mouth. Well, old Grace used to come into Yum Yum's.

'Now, of course, you can imagine, old Custard couldn't stand her. She usually had enough money for a cup of tea or two. He'd make her sit in the back corner of the bar where no one could see her. She used to sit and talk to herself, saying, "I told her where to put it. I ain't taking that from no one. Portsmouth's a beautiful place. Nothing you can do about it mind . . . " And she'd chunter on like that.

'Well, when Custard was out, meeting his mates in the Cavalry or something, we used to slip her a quick Yum Yum and she used to sit and eat it like a half-starved camel. Well, Grace was a scavenger, spending her time combing through the dustbins outside the caffs. So it was while we were all going down with the hedgehogs, during the heatwave, old Grace disappeared. She didn't come into the shop for her tea and Yum Yum on the side for a few days. And then suddenly, one day, the kids from the

Goldern Lantern Chinese came in saying Grace was stuck in a pipe.

'It was my dinner hour so I told them to take me to see. I followed them down an alley that went behind the shops, you know, where they pile up all the old crates, bottles and packing cases. By the side of a shed there was some building stuff – bricks, gutters, drain covers, and a big concrete pipe, the kind they put in adventure playgrounds for kids to crawl through. Well, old Grace had crawled into this one and covered herself over with cardboard boxes like she usually does. She was face down, her hair all sticky with bits of paper and leaves stuck in it.

'"There," said one of the kids. "There she is."

'I knew immediately something was wrong. Even

people asleep aren't that still and quiet. I bent down and moved her head. She was dead, poor old Grace. There she was, her eyes half open, half shut, her face all grey and her skin covered with tiny bits of gravelly stuff off the concrete pipe. Then I saw her lips. Round her mouth was the dried up stains of Monument Valley Mix. I nearly threw up.

'I covered her over with one of her bits of cardboard, and I found myself crying for her. The two kids were standing there looking at me and at her. I don't think they could believe it. I mean they were shocked such a thing could happen to an old woman. So I told them not to worry, and I'd tell the police. They didn't say anything else, but I can bet you they did when they got in. They had an old granny themselves who used to sit in the back in the Golden Lantern and they knew for sure *she* wouldn't end up face down in a concrete pipe out the back of some shops.

'Of course, when I told the rest, back at the ranch, everyone was very sad and all that, but no one asked *how* she died. I think people thought she was half dead anyway and it could have been something she picked up off one of those birds she let feed off her lips. No one could possibly want to do her in for anything she'd got in her polythene bags. No: she'd died in her sleep, and it hadn't been cold. This was during the hot spell.

'Well, I was standing there telling Rosetta about old Grace and I got that feeling again. It couldn't be the Yum Yums could it? I suddenly felt kind of ashamed. As if *I* had done her in by giving her Yum Yums. Killed her with kindness. I felt terrible. I mean even *more* terrible, what with the stomach cramps and the heat and everything.

'I had to tell someone. Maeve! My great mate at Yum Yum's was an Irish girl called Maeve. I've never seen anyone look so proper and yet come out with the things she did. She'd stand there so straight and calm-looking, and she'd start talking about old Custard. "Hell will be too nice a place for him. If only we had a few hundred Sioux Indians here . . . "

'She got up to some terrible tricks, too. It was her who put the glasses and moustache on John Wayne's face on the poster up on the wall in Yum Yum's, and I think it was her who changed the sign on the toilets. It said "Guys" over one and "Dames" over the other, but she put another notice over the top of "Guys" so it said "Horses". The next day men were going out to the toilets and coming back into the bar saying, "Oi, where's the toilets in this place?" You should have seen Custard's face when he went out and had a look. You'd've thought someone had nicked his toy gun.

'Anyway, I told Maeve everything I thought about the Yum Yums and poor old Grace. Maeve had a think. She was very practical. She just said:

'"Well my dear, we'd best find out where these Yum Yum thingummies come from."

'The boxes that they came in had no writing on at all, so that told us nothing. None of us ever got to see the books – Custard kept them locked away in his fort! The only thing to do was to suss out delivery time. Junior was the lad who did the heavy stuff round the place. So Maeve and me nobbled him.

'"I'll check it out for you, babes," he said. I can't stand that "babes" business, but you don't complain when you're asking favours, do you?

'Well, that wasn't much use either. Junior said there was no name on the side of the truck and the driver had no uniform or anything, so that told us nothing. All the boxes were plain covered. We were stumped.

'Maeve and me sat at a table in our afternoon break next to John Wayne's legs up there on the wall, trying to figure out what to do.

'"I know," said Maeve, "stow away."

'"Stow away?" I said. "Where? Where?"

'"In the truck, of course. In the delivery truck," she said. And she was serious. She had a lovely way of looking at you straight in the eye.

'"Stow away," she says.

'And I thought, "Hell, why not?"

'So this is how it happened.

'We told Junior to tell us when the next delivery was due and we told him exactly what he had to do.

'About a week later, Junior comes rushing in:

'"I'm on an unloading job right now. If you've got plans, then now's the time."

'Custard was in his fort doing his "paperwork" as he used to call it. Junior was unloading the boxes. So Maeve and me are hiding behind the back door, waiting for Junior to give us the signal. We're waiting for him to get the driver into his cab. He does it and tips us the wink, and we're out the back door and slip into the back of the truck. Junior closes the doors, but he doesn't lock them. He bangs twice on the back.

'"OK, you're away," he shouts to the driver and we were off.

'I couldn't believe we were doing it. Sitting in the back of the truck going who-knows-where? And that Maeve, she's sitting there as calm as if she was on a bus. Well, heaven knows how long that trip was. The thing was, the driver, he had a little window in the back of his cab so that he could see into his truck. Of course it was dark, but Maeve was forever sitting up and looking out trying to make out where we were. She goes, "I think this is Willesden." Then she goes, "I know where we are – Clapham" which is right over the other side of London. Then she goes, "We're in Hackney now." And that's right over the other side from Clapham, isn't it? And all the time there was this smell. The smell of old Yum Yum Burgers. Can you imagine, locked up in prison with a mouldy Yum Yum Burger?

'Anyway, we drive on and on. Finally, the truck stops. The driver gets out. I stopped breathing.

'"This is it," I thought. "We're going to be found out now. He's going to open the doors, and here we are looking like a pair of spare lemons.

'We listened, and his footsteps went away. Where were we?

'"OK girl," says Maeve. "What are we going to do?"

'"Well, let's take a butchers."

'We opened the door just a little bit and peeped out. We were in some kind of back yard.

'We could see it was piled high with old boxes: cardboard ones, wooden ones. I was just about to open the door a bit more when a feller came out. I pulled the door back. I just had time to see him. He had an old white coat on and it was covered in old blood. Spots, splodges and smears of it. He had a box in his hand: he chucked it on to one of the piles and went back inside.

'"OK," I said. "It's now or never." We jumped out the back of the truck, hopped across the yard and hid behind some of the boxes. I looked at Maeve's face.

'"Where are we, for heaven's sake?" she whispered.

'"Search me," I said.

'"What is this place?"

'"I don't know," I said.

'The yard smelled like pig-bins. Awful. Rotting dinners.

'"They don't make Yum Yum Burgers *here*, do they?" I said.

'"Well, they don't make paper aeroplanes, do they?"

'Then I caught sight of something. It was a bit of paper sticking out between two boxes. I looked at what was written on it: "George Watson and Sons Limited – Animal Disposal and Pet Food Supplies". Underneath was a little picture of a horse and a donkey standing side by side. Below this was printed like a bill, you know, with money. I handed it to Maeve. That piece of paper said everything. Custard was buying up meat from a knacker's yard, where they kill old donkeys and horses and stuff, and shipping it to this place to turn into hamburgers, instead of its going into pet food.

'"He could be put away for this," says Maeve.

'All I could think of was poor old Grace. I just stared at that little tiny picture of the horse and the donkey. Then Maeve was there:

'"Hey, have a look at this, will you?"'

'It was another one of those bits of paper. On this one it says, "Outback Foods Limited, Russ Mackay, Sydney, Australia". And on this one there's a little black-and-white picture as well. And cross my heart sure to die, if it isn't a picture of a blessed kangaroo. I didn't know whether to laugh or cry. We were standing in the back yard of a place where dead horses, donkeys and kangaroos went in and hamburgers came out. Amazing!

'We had blown Custard's whole little game. The truck with nothing written on the side, the plain cardboard boxes. Everything blown, with two bits of paper.

'For Maeve, though, that wasn't enough:

'"We've got to get a closer look at this place." And she pointed to the side of the building.

'There was a row of dirty little windows all along the wall by some bins and plastic bags and stuff, right? We made a dash for it so as not to be spotted and got to the side of the building. Maeve climbed up onto one of the bins and looked in.

'"What can you see?" I asked.

'She didn't answer. Next she climbed down from the bin and her face was white. Like all the colour had been wiped out of it. Well, I was just about to climb up on the bin myself, but looking at her face held me back for a moment. Then out of the corner of my eye, I saw something move. Coming round the end of the building was one of those men in their white overalls covered in blood.

'"He's got a meat axe in his hand," Maeve shouts, and we ran. We belted down the alley by the side of the building, and at the end there was this fence right in front

of us. We looked back and the bloke with the meat axe was climbing over the bins, coming for us. Then Maeve took one more look at the fence and kicked. She gave about three big kicks and a panel in the fence fell out. She shoved me through, climbed through herself and we were in someone's back yard.

'This awful place backed onto someone's house. Just imagine it. Living next door to somewhere they mashed up dead donkeys! Standing in the back yard was an old feller looking at his pigeons. Well, he *had* been looking at his pigeons, before we burst in. By the time we got there, the pigeons were all around him and he was staggering back with them flying all over the place.

'We didn't give him time to see anything else. Maeve pushed me down this alley beside the house. We ran down there, through this little gate and into the street.

'By now I was thinking, "There could be two of them after us. The feller with the meat axe and the feller with the pigeons. Well, I tell you, I didn't dare look over my shoulder. Down the street we went, running hell for leather. Round the corner, and there was a row of shops. The first was a junk shop. We took one look at it and we were in, and there we were, panting for all our worth, pretending to look at old electric fires and secondhand comics.

'I was dying to turn round and look through the window. Any second now, I imagined I'd see two men running past with pigeons and meat axes flying round them.

'Well, after that,' said the Bakerloo flea woman to me, 'there's not much more to tell you.'

'What do you mean?' I said.

'Well, that's it. You know everything now.'

'Hang on,' I said. 'Did anyone catch you?'

'Oh, no. They never caught us. I wouldn't be here to tell you if they had, would I?' she said.

'And you never told me what Maeve saw through the window.'

'Do you know?' she said, 'I've never found out. Maeve never told me. Many's the time I asked her, but she's never said. I've just had to imagine it.'

'And what about the Yum Yum Burger Bar?'

'Well,' said the Bakerloo flea woman, 'The day after we got back to Yum Yum's we told everyone, before Custard swaggered in at his usual time. There was talk all over the place about what to do. The police? The health people? Everything. A walk-out by all of us?

'Well, while all this was going on, and people were shouting and getting excited all over the place, Maeve was writing all over the walls and windows with a whack-ing great felt-tip pen. Things like: "Don't touch the Donkeyburgers" and "We serve Kangarooburgers here". Can you imagine Custard's face when he walked in that morning? It was a case of Custard's Last Stand.

'You remember, old General Custer was the bloke who was surrounded by Indians and finished off. We told him we weren't working another minute in the place till the Yum Yums had been looked at. So there was nothing he could say to that, and it wasn't long before *our* General Custard was surrounded by the council health people. The place was closed down. And that was that!'

The Bakerloo flea woman looked at me. Then she said:

'I was up that way a month ago. The shop where it was is a video place now and do you know what was in the window? You'll never guess. A big poster for "True Grit" with a giant picture of John Wayne standing there. I could have died.'

'Don't say that,' I said, and looked at my hamburger.

But she wasn't listening.

'There's my bus,' she said, and before I could say goodbye or anything else, she was out of the door and away.

I took one more look at my hamburger.

'I don't think I'll finish that just now,' I thought, and I walked out of the shop into the High Street.

Babygrow

I was walking through the Stratford Shopping Arcade. It's one of those big indoor places where there's Marks & Spencer's, Sainsbury's, Rumbelows, Mothercare and all. When you go up to the big car parks there are always kids having races in the Sainsbury trolleys. Well, I was walking past Mothercare and I saw someone who looked very much like the Bakerloo flea woman. 'What's she doing in Mothercare?' I thought.

I stood and watched her. 'Must be stuff for her grand-daughter or niece or someone,' I thought. 'I'll ask her when she comes out.'

She was buying up quite a load of stuff. Clothes, rattles and *piles* of plastic pants. Imagine what it must feel like walking around all day in them. Pretty steamy, I reckon. Anyway, when she had finished, paid and was leaving the shop I went over to her.

'Hello, it's me,' I said.

'Look, don't bother me now,' she said.

'It's all right, I wasn't going to,' I said. 'I was only saying hello.'

'I've got a lot on my mind,' she said. 'It's all very upsetting.'

'Oh, I'm sorry,' I said.

'Where I live,' she began, 'I'm on a balcony. There's ten flats to a balcony . . .'

'Look,' I said, 'I'm not stopping you, am I?'

'No, it won't take a moment.'

'Fine,' I said.

'Well, I'm on one end of the balcony and there's two sisters on the other end.'

Then she suddenly put her face close to mine:

'You won't breathe a word of this to anyone, will you?'

'No. Promise.' I said.

'This is a serious business. It's about a baby that died.'

'Look,' I said, 'I don't think I want to know about this.'

'Hang on, listen,' she said. 'These two sisters, right? Sharon and Lorraine – they're twins. They fell in love with the same feller – David. Terrible business, really. To tell you the truth, I don't think that David could choose between them, they were so alike. I mean if he thought the one of them was very nice, I can't think of a reason why he wouldn't think the other was just as nice.

'And as for them, well they just happened to think alike on this as well as all the other things they thought about. This time it was the same feller. And he *was* nice, even if I say so myself. A very smart dresser, lovely sense of humour and very good teeth. Lovely teeth.'

'Teeth?' I said. 'Teeth? What's teeth got to do with it?'

'Oh well, you wouldn't know, son,' she said.

'Anyway, lovely feller though he was, he was no angel. Both girls find out they're both expecting at the same time.'

'Expecting?' I said. 'Expecting what?'

'Expecting a baby of course.'

'Oh.'

'Well, you realize what that meant, do you?' she said.

'What?' I said.

'Well, he was the father of both the babies that were on the way.'

'Was he?' I said.

'Well, it was too much for him. He just couldn't face up to it. I think he had told both of them that he was going to marry them. One at a time of course. Maybe he had thought he'd make up his mind later, or something, and then events caught up with him. He must have spent a sleepless night over it and then he disappeared off the face of the Earth. There's men for you. Well, if it was one sleepless night for him, it was a hundred for Sharon and Lorraine. Each.

'So there they were, each expecting a child. I think they were a great help to each other, to tell the truth. I mean they could talk about all their aches and pains and

all the trips to the Health Centre, and all the worries that
you have about the baby's going to be dead or it's going to
have a bit missing or be damaged, or how the birth's going
to be really hard. And there's always someone round
your way who's got some horror story about things
going wrong, too early, too late, wrong way up and all
that.

'Well, I say all that because they hadn't really called on
me at all yet in all this. I didn't come into it. I mean, I
could *see* what was happening. So, anyhow, they have
their babies. And blow me, they're both girls – and
something else. Of course, they look almost identical.
Well, they would, wouldn't they? So here are these two
twins with the same baby. Except there's two of them.
Babies, I mean. Well, of course, it was the talk of the flats.
I mean, it was quite something looking at them going out.
The pair of them almost became local celebrities. Everyone felt they had the right to have a look – you know,
even old fellers who don't talk to anyone except their dogs
were trying to sneak a look.

'Then something awful happened. To tell the truth, to
this day I don't know exactly what, but I'll tell it you as
best I can from what I've been told.

'The two women, Sharon and Lorraine, slept in the
same room with the babies so as they could share the
feeding and changing in the middle of the night. So one
night one of them was on, and the next night it was the
other. Up changing nappies, doing the bottles – all that.
It meant that they each got a bit of sleep. Very sensible.
Then one night, Sharon was on while Lorraine was
asleep. And one of the babies dies.

'Sharon wakes Lorraine up and says:

'"Lorraine, Lorraine, she's stopped breathing."

'So Sharon's up and they're trying to make the poor little thing breathe. And they're crying, and trying the kiss of life, anything. It's no use: the poor thing's dead.

'But which baby is it?

'Sharon says to Lorraine that it's Lorraine's baby that's died. But Lorraine looks at both the babies and says it isn't. She says the dead baby is Sharon's. So now the tears start all over again.

'Well, I don't know what put it in their minds, but next thing one of them's knocking on my door – at three o'clock in the morning. So I'm up in my dressing-gown going, "Who is it? Who is it?"

'And one of them's calling through the letterbox:

'"It's Lorraine. Can you come quick?"'

'Well, you don't ask questions at moments like that. I was out the door, down the balcony and in at her flat.

'There was the poor little dead one lying on the bed and there was Sharon cuddling the other one in her arms. Of course, I immediately picked up the dead one thinking I could save her somehow. I patted her back, squeezed her little chest to try and get her to take air in. But she had an awful limp feel about her, heavy in your hands. I saw it was useless and Lorraine was getting hysterical.

'Now, at this point, I wasn't really listening to what Lorraine was screaming about, thinking it was all about her baby being lost and everything, but suddenly I picked up what she was saying.

'"It's not my baby. It's hers. Hers. Give me back my baby. Make her give me mine."

'I looked at Sharon and she just shook her head. For a moment it seemed clear. Lorraine had gotten herself into such a state that she was now imagining that Sharon had like swapped the babies over or something – that Sharon had found her own baby dead, and then made out that it was Lorraine's. I looked at the babies' clothes. They were both the same.

'But then, I thought, maybe it's true. Maybe Lorraine's not imagining it. Maybe Sharon was holding Lorraine's baby. So I looked at Sharon and I said:

'"Did you? Did you change the babies over?"

'"Of course I didn't," she said.

'"Look," I said, "we haven't got time to argue like this. We've got to ring the doctor."

'"But my baby's not dead," says Lorraine, and she wails.

'The whole thing felt like an awful dream. It was dark, Lorraine screaming, the dead baby lying there.

'And while I was standing in that room, I had a funny feeling I'd heard this argument all before. As if I'd heard someone telling me all this before. How someone had to decide which of the two women was telling the truth. And that person drew a circle on the floor or something and made the two women stand on opposite sides of the circle and try and drag the child out of the circle onto their side. Like a tug-of-war. The trouble was, as I thought that – and it went through my mind in a flash – I couldn't remember who won. I mean, I found myself thinking, did the judge say that the woman who pulled the hardest was the true mother because it showed her love was the strongest? Or did he say the mother was the one who was afraid to pull in case she hurt the child? As I say, all this went through my mind in a flash. Were we going to ring the doctor or decide now?

'The baby was lost. I knew enough about the business to see that. She was already cold. I couldn't bear the thought of a doctor coming in just at that second with people's feelings running as high as that. So I said something completely mad:

'"I'll tell you how we'll find out whose baby it is. Give her here."

'And amazing though it may seem, Sharon handed her over. I looked at this baby, creasing up its little face and blinking. I think for one moment they thought *I* was going to make off with it. I think for one moment *I* thought I was.

'"Right," I said. "I'll hold the baby and one of you take

its arms, one of you take its legs and whoever pulls the hardest will be the mother."

'I watched their two faces. Sharon stepped forward to take her arms, but Lorraine just said:

'"You must be crazy. You're mad. How can you expect me to pull my baby to pieces?"

'Now of course I had no intention of getting them to do any such thing. I wanted to see how they would react. And sure enough one went one way, and the other went another. So I looked at Sharon.

'"Lorraine's the mother," I said.

'"What?" she says. "What? What are you talking about?"

'"Lorraine said as she couldn't bear to see the child harmed. You were going to come in for the tug-of-war . . ."

'"Don't be daft. You're crazy. 'Course I was going to go in there and tug. I wasn't going to give her away, was I?"

'Suddenly that had me stumped. I had put my big foot right in it. I had sided with Lorraine but maybe I was right. Maybe I was wrong. I breathed in for a moment. I was still holding the baby, so I says to Sharon:

'"Ring the doctor."

'The phone was by the bed. By the time she'd made the call, I'd time to think again. It was like doing my sums. Before, there'd been two women, sharing two babies, living together, going about together and sharing all the jobs. Now there were two women and one baby. What now?

'"Look you two," I said. "There's only one way out of this. The baby belongs to both of you. You did it before

when there was two of them, you can do it again now there's one, can't you?"

'There was no answer from either of them.

'"It's either that or you'll kill each other."

'Well, I looked from one to the other and back again. Was that a look of relief on Sharon's face that I hadn't found out she had stolen it, or was it a look that meant, "At least Lorraine will stop trying to get my baby off me", or was she just glad that here was a chance they could stop arguing? And Lorraine's face. She had stopped crying and nearly smiled through it. Not quite. Did that mean she didn't have to go on pretending her story was true, or that at least she had the share of *some* of a child, or what?

'But whatever, they both seemed in that moment to think it was possible. They could share the child. I went on holding the baby. The two of them covered the dead child and by then the other one needed feeding and changing and somehow it seemed like as it was all we could do. Heating the milk, doing the nappy. By the time we were halfway through that, the doctor was there and told us what we knew already.

'So here am I in Mothercare buying up some more gear for the little thing.'

'Well,' I said. 'How's it going? The sharing?'

'Well,' she says. 'Not very well.'

'Why not?'

She laughs. 'Because it's between the three of us now.'

'What does that mean?' I said.

'Oh, only that I keep an eye on them. Hoping for all my worth that it'll work out. You see, if I buy the stuff like

this, the one can't blame the other it's the wrong stuff.
They can blame me instead.'

So I looked at what the Bakerloo flea woman had got.

A kind of yellow all-in-one thing.

'What's that?' I said.

'A babygrow,' she says.

'Sounds like something you put on the garden,' I said.

'I hope they like it, that's all. I must get back. Bye for
now.' She was off and I was left standing there reeling
from it all.

Then I thought, she didn't tell me what the baby's
called. I was about to run after her, but I wasn't sure
whether she'd gone down the subway or over to the High
Street.

So I was stood there wondering – which one *was* the
mother? Or maybe it doesn't matter.

Maureen

I was in London Zoo the other day, I've got a season ticket and I like to look at the animals when no one else is there. Like in winter. Have you seen the polar bear? It paces to and fro along this rock and then every now and then it dives into the freezing water. You'd die if you went in there. When it gets out, it shakes all the water off. I was watching this when I heard a voice behind me:

'Have you seen my mate over there?'

I looked around and it was the Bakerloo flea woman.

'Oh hello,' I said. 'I was just looking at the polar bear.'

'You ought to take a gander at the grizzlies,' she said. My mate's in there.'

'Oh,' I said. 'You know one of the zoo keepers, do you?'

'No,' she says.

'Who's your mate, then?' I asked.

'One of the grizzlies,' she says.

'Oh, yes. And what's he called?'

'Maureen.'

'Right then,' I said. 'Take me to meet her.'

So off we went, past those goat things with the twisty horns and that horrible vulture that stands there ripping at bits of old flesh. Actually, its neck looks like bits of old flesh as well. Over to the grizzlies. The grizzly bears.

'There she is. Maureen,' she called to her, 'Maureen! Maureen!'

And there in the corner of the bears' pen is a great big grizzly. I looked at it. Its eyes rolled over towards us.

'See', said the Bakerloo flea woman, 'she knows me.'

'Knows you, my foot,' I said. 'She does that to everyone. Watch this. What's she called, did you say? Maureen?'

'That's it,' she says.

'Right,' I said. 'MAUREEN! MAUREEN!'

Well, all Maureen did at that was lick her foot.

'See,' said the Bakerloo flea woman. 'She only looks up for me.'

'All right,' I said. 'How do you know her then?'

'Now you're asking,' she says. 'You're not going to stand here in the freezing cold and hear this one out, are you? Let's go over to the café.'

So off we went, past the gorillas sulking in their house, past the gibbons whooping around like kids gone mad in an adventure playground. We went into the café and we were the only people there apart from a young couple looking into each other's eyes and trying to drink one cup of coffee at the same time.

'Let's see,' she says. 'Maureen. Well, it all starts with the buses. You see, old Maureen, she nearly got run over by one.'

'By a bus?' I said.

'Yep,' she said.

'They don't drive buses round the zoo, do they?' I said.

'No. In London. A double-decker bus in the Holloway Road.'

I tried to picture it. A huge grizzly bear walking across the Holloway Road with a double-decker bus zooming past it. No. Couldn't be true.

'You see, son,' she said, 'I was a clippy – bus conductress to you – on the number 43, among others. On this particular day the crew was me and Lloyd. A day much like any other, coming down the Holloway Road. Shopping day for many round the old Holloway Arcade, Jones Brothers and all that, under the railway bridge at Holloway Road Station. I was on top, on the upper deck, right up the front, collecting the fares off about five kids who were busy driving the bus to Mars or somewhere. Then there's this big kid, easily fifteen, with the younger ones and he says:

'"Half to Highbury Corner."

'"You're never a half," I says.

'"Am," he goes.

'"Come on, son. Don't mess me about." And I held out my hand and did my I'm-getting-fed-up look out the window.

'Well, just as I looked up, I saw in front of us this whopping great big lorry. Nothing strange in that, except just as I am looking at it, the back doors slowly open out towards us. And, just as I'm thinking Lloyd's going to give the lorry-driver a flash on his lights or something, this great fat grizzly bear rolls out the back of the lorry on to the Holloway Road. Right in front of us.

'Of course, the kids went spare.

'"It's a bear. IT'S A BEAR!" And it certainly weren't no man dressed up. First thing it does is stand up on its rear legs and it looks about ten foot tall. Then it opens its mouth in a great big yawn and you can see right down its throat – teeth, tongue, tonsils, the lot. It must have been about two foot from Lloyd's nose, in the cab down below me.

'Of course, everyone on top with me is crowding to the front of the bus. They all want to get a sight of it.

'"It's a bear. It's a bear," they keep shouting.

'Well, of course, it didn't just stand there. It turned. Maybe it thought it could get back into the lorry, but the doors had swung back. Of course, the fellers driving the lorry knew nothing about it.

'But then it starts loping up by the side of the lorry. Can you imagine, sitting in the cab of a lorry thinking you've got a grizzly bear safe and sound in the back when suddenly it's standing there looking at you through the window? Well, that didn't last long. Next thing it does is cross the road towards Holloway Road Station.

'By now, there's cars hooting and people screaming and the road is clearing like a bomb's about to go off. Cars are reversing down the Holloway Road, up the Holloway Road, and people are jumping off my bus and scarpering. Off they went, some of them leaving behind their bags of fruit and veg and what-have-you. They'd probably have been safer staying on board. I think it was the sight of everybody else bunking off that got them going. Once two or three were running, so was the rest. Most of them belted off down beside the college there. The fellers driving the lorry pulled into the side and got out.

'For a moment it seemed like it was just them, us and the bear. I was downstairs by now. I looked behind us and

saw it was one of those days that the buses get all clogged up together. There was about four or five of us, not all 43s of course, standing there.

'The grizzly by now had lurched back to our side of the road again. Well, I'll never know what made Lloyd do it but, blow me, if he doesn't start the bus running forwards towards the bear. And the moment he does that, I'm shouting to Frank in the bus behind who must have known what was going on by now.

'"Follow us," I shouted. "We can trap it."

'Goodness knows what made me say it. And goodness knows what made Frank agree, but there's now two buses making off down the Holloway Road after this huge great big grizzly bear.

'Well, like I said, the road's clear by now. But the sight of these two giant red buses coming up to it sent the bear off down the road. On we went, the other buses following behind, trundling along after the bear, down the Holloway Road. And the third and fourth buses are spreading out across the road and we're taking up the whole Holloway Road, both sides, and the old bear is loping along ahead of us.

'On we went, past the Brewery Tap – that's a pub. "It's not going to poke its nose in there, is it," I thought, "and go 'Half a lager, mate'?" No, on it went. Past the old Arsenal Café that isn't there any more. "It's not going to go in *there* is it? You know a bit of the old 'Cuppa tea, mister,' 'Sorry, we don't serve Spurs supporters or bears.'" No none of that either.

'On it went. Past the kebab joints – without stopping for a quick doner. And there's people cowering in the doorways of their shops, looking out of windows. You'd've thought we was the Queen.

'And that old bear looks like it's enjoying itself. I mean it's really getting a chance to stretch its old legs. It's moseying up to the "Keep Left" sign on the island in the middle of the road. Next, it's ambled across the road to poke its nose into the big catering place. Probably saw its reflection in the window, but for one moment it looked like it was going to go in there and order a hundred and forty dinners for a wedding reception or something.

'Then as we trundle on down towards it, it comes to the big motor-cycle shop. "Maybe it's going to hop on a Honda next," I thought. Imagine it, a grizzly bear zooming down the Holloway Road on a Honda. Then, before we know it, we're at Highbury Corner. Now, Highbury Corner, I don't know whether you know it, it's not really a corner at all. It's a great big roundabout. The CB people call it Highbury Doughnut. In the middle, there's like a little park. Trees, grass, bushes, flowers and stuff. So there's us coming down past Highbury and Islington Station. People rushing into the Post Office to hide, running off to Highbury Fields.

'And, of course, the same thing's happening up the streets that feed into Highbury Corner. Cars are turning round and reversing away. People are getting into safe places to watch and the buses are left standing there. Well, I don't know if it was the sight of our four or five buses coming down the Holloway Road together, or what, but the buses down all the other roads, Upper Street and all that, they start moving in towards the big Highbury Corner roundabout as well.

'So suddenly there's about twelve of us. Twelve double-decker buses. Well the old bear must have thought something was happening because it was like we was surrounding that park space in the middle. A great red ring of buses.

'Now, there's a fence round the roundabout. And what with our buses closing in and the sight of the green leaves and flowers on the roundabout, the bear climbs the fence and was in. I don't suppose the men from the Council ever thought when they were building that fence that it'd have to stand the weight of a two-ton grizzly.

'Anyway, the grizzly bear was on the inside and we were on the outside. What I didn't know, though, was that those two fellers driving the truck that had the bear in had hopped on one of our buses. Somewhere along the line the police had got to hear of it, all the fire services and the zoo emergency people, and for all I know there was a gang of SAS men on red alert, RAF helicopters and goodness knows what.

'Next thing, the drivers and the keepers are at the fence, looking in. The bear had quietened down by now, it was just snuffling about in the bushes. One of the keepers was calling out to it. That was the first time I heard its name.

'"Maureen," he goes. "Maureen."

'I thought "Maureen"? Now, you'd never have known it was Maureen to look at her, would you? Fancy that.

'Well, not long after that, the zoo people did their bit with them drug pellets, and the old bear keeled over and went to sleep. And that was the end of that.

'They *had* to shoot the pellets. I mean no one was going

to go up to it and say, "Look here Maureen, would you like to walk back to your lorry now? Sorry the doors fell open, but we'll lock them next time . . . "

'They had to get this thing like a breakdown-truck to hoist her up and stick her in the lorry. To tell the truth I didn't stick around to see all that, but I'm told it took about twenty grown men to push old Maureen in there. Then they carted her off to the zoo, here. Of course, the papers next day were full of it. MAUREEN'S DAY OUT and MAUREEN'S REMOVALS and there were pictures of her being hoisted into the truck.

'Sad to say, none of them got the picture I wanted to see. It would have been from high-up: a picture of Highbury Corner surrounded with all our buses and in the middle old Maureen, snuffling through the council flower beds. I mean it was us in our buses that cornered it, wasn't it? All the rest was drug-guns and breakdown-trucks and all. Oh well, not to worry, I'll just have to carry the picture of it round in my head. I can always come in here and have a look at her.'

'That's very nice,' I thought.

'It'll break my heart when she dies, mind,' she said.

'Look,' I said, 'I've got to go. I'm going to have one more look at her myself, now you've told me all this. You coming?'

I went off to look at Maureen. I was standing there looking at her when the keeper came out of the little door of the bear's pen.

'You've been feeding Maureen, have you?' I asked.

He looked at me and said:

'You what?'

'You've been feeding Maureen, have you?'

'No,' he said. 'I've been feeding the bears.'

'Well, isn't that one Maureen?' I said.

'No,' he said. 'That's Samson.'

'What about that one?' I said, pointing to the other one.

'That's Betty,' he said.

'Well, where's Maureen?'

'You tried the shop, sir? People who get lost often go there, sir.'

I suddenly realized he thought I was some kind of a nutter.

'Have you ever looked after a bear in here called Maureen?' I said.

'Not in the last six years, we haven't. I'm sorry sir, I can't hang about.' And off he went. He was probably glad to get away.

I went back to where the Bakerloo flea woman was. I was going to tell her it wasn't Maureen. It was Samson and Betty. But she wasn't there.

'Oh well,' I thought. 'Just as well. It wouldn't be right somehow to tell her that her bear wasn't really the same one that fell off the back of a lorry. Unless . . . unless she'd made the whole thing up. No she wouldn't have. Everything else she's told me is true, isn't it?' I said to myself . . .